frostie
THE DEADMAN

frostie THE DEADMAN

zackary richards

Nicholas K. Burns Publishing
Utica, New York

Nicholas K. Burns Publishing
130 Proctor Boulevard
Utica, New York 13501

First Edition

ISBN 0–9713069–8–2

Library of Congress Cataloging-in-Publication Data

Richards, Zackary, 1952-

Frostie the deadman / Zackary Richards.-- 1st ed.

p. cm.

Summary: Ten-year-old Winks and thirteen-year-old Josh inadvertently
bring a serial murderer back to life when they use his hat and scarf to dress
a snowman for a winter carnival, freeing him to seek revenge against the
vigilantes who killed him.

ISBN 0-9713069-8-2 (pbk.)

[1. Serial murderers--Fiction. 2. Murder--Fiction. 3. Snowmen--Fiction.
4. Heroes--Fiction. 5. Haunted places--Fiction. 6. Adirondack Mountains
(N.Y.)--Fiction. 7. Horror stories.] I. Title.

PZ7.R39413Fr 2004

[Fic]--dc22

2004013615

This book is dedicated to
Alice R. Maher

Simply the best

1

THIRTY YEARS AGO

It was almost midnight. The air was cold and crisp with white billowy clouds sailing across the wintry sky. The giant evergreens of the Adirondack Mountains swayed gently in the breeze, their icy branches sparkling under the light of the full moon. The air was thick with the smell of pine, birch, and cedar. Stars covered the sky.

In the valley below, the wind skipped across the frozen lake like a playful child and danced with the cheery-faced snowmen that the townspeople placed upon its surface. Smoke from wood burning stoves poured from the chimneys of the surrounding houses. Snow devils twirled around fence posts while cornfields and cow pastures lay sleeping under a blanket of snow. In the distance, a coydog howled.

And in the midst of this rural splendor, high in the mountains, the cold eyes of Lucas Walks peered out from the darkness.

Crouched behind the shadow of a fallen tree, he studied the four men as they tracked him up the side of Thunderclap Mountain. As their flashlights blinked behind the crowded pines, Walks' fingers tightened around the broken tree limb that he would use as a weapon.

The man with the pale blue eyes could feel Walks watching. They all could. They were in his element now and it came as no surprise when Lucas' footprints began to disappear into the brush and the frozen forest floor.

One of the men turned. "Tracks are gone. Now what do we do?"

The blue-eyed man carefully surveyed the surrounding area. "No doubt he wants us to split up," he said. "And I don't see where we have a choice but.... I got an idea. Listen...."

Lucas grinned as the four separated. Within minutes, one of the men was in range, fumbling his way through the dense underbrush. Walks' face grew taut and his eyes began to resemble two black marbles. He could barely contain the excitement welling up inside him.

The tracker approached slowly and cautiously, swinging his flashlight in long arcs. As he pressed forward into the darkness, the wind rattled the tree branches above him like old bones. His heartbeat quickened.

Easy now, he told himself. *There are four of us and only one of him. Just remember, if he tries....*

Something moved!

He spun the flashlight in full circle but saw nothing. Had he imagined it? No! He was sure he had heard...seen someth....

Suddenly, Walks was in front of him, grinning like a Jack-o-Lantern.

"Hi ya, buddy!"

Before the man could make a sound, something flashed past the corner of his eyes. Pain rocketed across the side of his head and stars swirled before him. His legs began slipping and his arms flailed wildly in an almost cartoon-like fashion.

He was struck again, this time in the chest. His breath exploded from his lungs and he collapsed to the ground.

Under the light of the full moon, he saw Lucas staring down. His teeth were clenched and saliva dangled from his chin. His eyes were wild, like that of a rabid animal. Walks was lost in the moment. Lost in the passion. He raised the club to deliver the final, fatal blow.

Oh, if I only had more time to savor this, Walks thought. *To drink in this wonderful moment!*

Suddenly, Lucas was struck from behind. His club went sailing and his legs buckled. He was struck again, hard, and descended into the darkness.

When Lucas awoke, he found himself bound hand and foot. As he jerked himself into a sitting position, a noose was quickly jammed over his head and pulled tight. Walks' eyes widened.

"You better not do this!!" he said in a rasping, yet threatening voice. "I have friends. Powerful friends!"

The man with the pale blue eyes crouched in front of him. "Men like you have no friends. Any last words?"

Walks said nothing.

The man nodded and turned to the others. "Hang him!"

"Wait! Wait!" Walks coughed. "Listen to me, all of you. You are going to regret this more than you can possibly imagine. Even if I have to crawl back from the deepest pit in hell itself," he said, eyeing each one of them. "I will have my revenge on you all!"

The blue-eyed man joined the others and began to pull. "We'll be waiting."

2

PRESENT DAY

PRESENT DAY

In the uppermost region of Adirondack County, 18 miles south of the Canadian border, lies the town of Sparks, New York. It's a quiet little community known for its lush green hillsides, cool streams, and fresh mountain air.

Souvenir shops dot the main streets and ragtime bands play afternoon concerts in the park. People are friendly and tourists are made to feel welcome and at home. In the center of it all is a beautiful body of water known as Little Pond Lake. Together with the surrounding area's natural beauty and its friendly homespun appeal, Sparks exudes a rustic charm all its own.

Being so far north, winter weather usually arrives in late November and lasts through the better part of April. About 150 inches of snow falls there each year making it the perfect place for a winter festival. Sparks held its first about forty-five-years ago and has continued the yearly tradition ever since. It is an event they proudly call the Snowman's Parade.

Back in the mid-1940s, someone (no one quite remembers who) suggested a contest be held to see who could build the best and most colorful snowman. All the townspeople were asked to participate. The prize was ten dollars and a free meal at a local restaurant, which at the time was considered quite generous. The event was to be held on Little Pond Lake.

It had been a particularly harsh winter and people were tired of being cooped up in their homes. Not only did they welcome the idea of a community event, they embraced it. Word traveled fast and by the day of the contest, nearly everyone in town had signed up.

The local dairy farmers provided horse drawn sleighs for transportation. The Women's League brought food, beverages, and blankets and the Salvation Army donated the hats and scarves for the snowmen. To keep warm they built fires inside empty fifty-gallon oil drums, passed around hot cider, and danced to music provided by a local jug band. As the evening drew to a close, the townspeople gathered and sang such favorites as "White Christmas" and "Jingle Bells."

They built over forty snowmen that night and the Best Snowman Contest wound up being the most successful event in the town's history.

As the years went by and the surrounding towns grew, the people of Sparks began to look for something that would attract tourists and put their little town on the map.

Since the Best Snowman Contest had been such a success, they expanded on the idea, turned it into a winter-long festival, and renamed it the Snowman's Parade.

No longer would the snowmen be placed randomly on the ice. Instead, they would be lined up in rows to resemble a marching band, outfitted with band jackets and plastic instruments, and maintained by the crews of the Department of Public Works.

The snowmen were positioned to face Shore Road. This way tourists driving through town would stop, take pictures, and hopefully spend a little money. The idea worked and every year since its inception the number of entries increased as did the number of people coming to see them.

At center stage was the Lead Snowman. Dressed in a neon blue jacket and holding a gold baton, it was placed in front to look as if it were indeed leading the parade.

In most instances, the snowman picked for that honor was the best built, the most attractive, and a virtual lock to win Best in Show. The present day prize was now one thousand dollars.

Sparks had come a long way over the years and everything associated with the parade—tee shirts, coffee mugs, ashtrays, bumper stickers, and banners—sold out quickly. Restaurants expanded, motels were built, and businesses flourished.

It was now mid-December and the Department of Public Works deemed Little Pond Lake sufficiently frozen to be safe. The contest rules stated that in order to be eligible for the Grand Prize, contestants must construct all entries at their residence and then transport them to the lake. Those that successfully made it to the parade in one piece were then registered, tagged, photographed, and assigned a temporary slot—the cut off date being fourteen days from the first major snowfall.

This year's first major snowfall arrived the day after Thanksgiving and it continued to snow off and on (mostly on) for the next ten days. According to the Committee rules, anyone who wanted to participate had only three days left.

3

It was Thursday afternoon, and the students from Sparks Central School were riding along old Route 511 on their way home.

The school bus was in its usual state of chaos. There was shouting, laughing, and crumpled papers flying overhead. Some kids made faces at the passing cars while others were content to sit back with their headphones and listen to the latest hit song at decibels that would shatter the windows at airport terminals. When things got too out of hand, the driver would hurl some meaningless threat that would quiet them down temporarily, but not long enough to make any real difference.

In the middle of it all was one kid who was having a particularly rough day. His name was Theodore "Winks" Shays. Winks was ten-years-old, had sandy blond hair, and a drooping left eyelid, the result of having gotten too close to his father's wood chipper without wearing protective goggles. He didn't mind the nickname; in fact, he preferred it to Theodore, but what he did hate was how his disability caused him to be singled out by nearly every bully in school.

Today, his problem was in the form of a big dim-witted thirteen-year-old by the name of Billy Curtis. Billy had taken Winks'

Superman loose-leaf binder from his book bag and was threatening to draw breasts on the "Man of Steel" with an indelible marker. Since the binder was Winks' most prized possession, he had no choice but to go to the back of the bus where Billy held court with his fellow sadists and beg for its return.

"C'mon, Billy, give it back!" Winks pleaded. "It belongs to me."

"It belongs to me," Billy repeated, mimicking his victim. "And what are you going to do if I don't? Use your superpowers on me?"

"Watch out, Billy," one of his companions said. "He might let you have it with his X-ray eye!"

Billy laughed, then winked at his friends as he popped the cap off his marker. Slowly, he lowered it to the binder, carefully watching the ten-year-old's face. Just before the tip touched the surface, Winks panicked, reached out, and tried to pull the binder from his tormentor's grasp, but Billy had anticipated the move and held tight. In retaliation, he grabbed the front of Winks' coat and flung him backward up the aisle where he fell to the floor. Winks' face reddened. His pratfall caught the attention of his fellow students who, along with Billy, burst out laughing. But Winks' humiliation wasn't over, not by a long shot.

Billy climbed out of his seat, lumbered toward Winks, and stood over him.

"Maybe I ought to make you eat this binder, wise guy," he said as he bent over and attempted to shove the object into Winks' face.

The boy struggled desperately as the binder came closer and closer.

Suddenly, a hand shot out from the seat beside them and grabbed Billy by the front of his coat.

"That's enough!"

Billy straightened up, pushed off the hand that held him, and

looked down to see who dared spoil his fun. Seeing an opportunity to add a new twist to his little game, Billy smiled, folded his
hands across his chest, and began bobbing his head up and down
like one of those dolls in the back of car windows.

"So," he said, "looks like we got a real tough guy here, don't
it, gang?" His friends nodded in agreement but made no attempt
to leave their seats. "You a tough guy, Campbell? Tough enough
to go one on one with me?"

"Yeah, you tell him, Billy!" one of his buddies shouted.

Billy turned and gave a knowing wink to his pals. "'Cause if
you are," he continued, "we can meet down at the lake at
say...four o'clock? Then we'll see just how tough you are."

Josh Campbell slowly rose from his seat and placed himself
directly in front of Billy Curtis.

"I'm not going to meet you at the lake," he said.

A huge grin came over Billy's face. "Oh, no?" he said, looking
back to make sure his friends weren't missing any of this. "What's
the matter, tough guy? Ain't got the guts?"

"Oh, I got the guts," Josh replied calmly. "The question is, do
you? Because if we're going to fight, we're going to do it right here
and right now."

Billy's eyes widened. No one had ever issued him such a chal-
lenge before.

"You mean here? On the school bus?"

"That's right," Josh said. "And if you start with me, I'll kick
your teeth so far down your throat, they'll have to pry my boot
from the back of your head with a crowbar."

The school bus became deadly quiet. No one had ever talked
to Billy Curtis like that. Some of the on-lookers actually pulled up
their book bags to cover themselves, fearing the inevitable explo-

sion between the two would send shrapnel flying in all directions.

Tiny beads of sweat appeared on Billy's forehead. Fight on the bus? You could be suspended, maybe even expelled. Was Campbell really crazy enough to risk that?

Billy looked closely into Josh's cold, green eyes and came back with the distinct impression that yes, he was.

Josh Campbell was only a few weeks short of thirteen himself. He was almost as tall as Billy and was built solidly enough to give the other boy a reason to be concerned. He had jet-black hair, slightly long, which he kept tucked behind his ears. He also had a reputation as a loner. Nobody really knew what Josh was capable of, and Billy wasn't sure he wanted to find out.

The silence was eventually noticed by the bus driver who, after taking a quick glance back, found the two boys standing toe to toe.

"Hey," he shouted. "You guys know better than to stand while the bus is in motion. Now take your seats, or I'll be forced to report the two of you."

Josh didn't budge. Instead, he continued to stare at Billy, daring him to make a move.

"I said sit down!" the driver repeated.

Not willing to risk expulsion and a possible beating, Billy backed off.

"I wouldn't dirty my hands on you, Campbell," he said finally. "And you!" he continued, flinging the binder at Winks. "Well, you better stay out of my way." With that, he lumbered back to his friends.

Josh calmly returned to his seat while Winks slid into the one beside him.

"Thanks," he said, tucking his binder back in his book bag. "If it weren't for you, I'd be spitting out pieces of plastic about now."

"Forget it," Josh replied and reopened the book he had been reading.

Although Josh and Winks were next-door neighbors, they didn't know each other all that well. Josh considered Winks a good but goofy kid with a bizarre fascination with comic book superheroes and much too young to hang out with. Still, the kid was harmless, and Josh couldn't stand to see that big jerk shove him around.

Josh tried to concentrate on his book but Winks' eyes continued boring into him.

"Hey, Josh, did you finish your entry for the Snowman's Parade yet? Me and my dad brought ours down to the lake last week."

Realizing that he wasn't going to get any reading done, Josh put down his book and shook his head. "No," he replied. "I haven't even started it. I've been too busy."

That wasn't really the truth, but Josh didn't want to let on that it was his father who was "too busy." As far back as Josh could remember, every year he and his dad would go out in the yard and build the Campbell snowman. It was almost a tradition. But things were different now. Several months ago, his father had purchased a small fuel oil company and his new responsibilities had him working nearly 'round the clock. This year it looked like Josh was on his own.

"I could help you," Winks said.

Josh was lost in thought and had no idea what Winks was referring to. "Help me what?"

"Help you build your snowman. Really, Josh, it would be my way of repaying you for taking care of Billy."

Josh wasn't crazy about the idea of having a ten-year-old hanging around him for the rest of the afternoon. "I don't think so, Winks," he said, slowly shaking his head. "Besides, committee rules say only one entry per family."

"I know, I know. And I'm not asking you to put my name on it or anything," he said, still trying to sell the idea. "All I'm saying is that I could help you build it. The committee doesn't have any rules against that. And together, we could have it finished in no time."

As much as Josh hated to admit it, Winks' suggestion did make a lot of sense. By himself, a snowman good enough and sturdy enough to make it to the parade would take at least a whole day to build, maybe a day and a half. But with Winks' help, he could probably wrap it up in a few hours. And since his father wasn't going to have any time to help....

"Okay, Winks," he said reluctantly, "it's a deal."

"Great!" the boy shouted. "C'mon, here's our stop."

4

As the two boys walked down the snow-covered street toward Josh's house, they swapped stories, occasionally threw snowballs at each other, and had contests to see who could slide the furthest on the patches of ice. In between, they planned the construction of the snowman, and how the work of rolling, packing, and shoveling would be split between them.

As they passed an old barn, Winks saw a large stalagmite hanging from a corner eave. "Hey, Josh," he said pointing. "Look at the size of that icicle. It would make a perfect 'backbone' for the snowman. Let's take it down and bring it to your house."

Josh shook his head. "I don't think so, Winks. I've decided not to use a 'backbone' this year."

Winks was clearly surprised. "Really? How come? My dad says putting one in the center keeps the snowman from falling apart during the ride to the lake."

Josh nodded. "My dad says the same thing but I don't buy it. Besides, did you ever notice that almost every snowman that has one starts looking ratty by the second week? Nah. As long as we pack the snow tightly enough we should be fine."

Winks shrugged and tossed up his hands. "Well, okay by me,

it's your snowman."

Time passed quickly and before long, they were at Josh's front door.

The Campbells lived in a big brown house that Josh's grandfather built. Josh's dad had grown up there back in the days when all the houses in the area, including his own, were dairy farms. That changed when the Milkways Company, a giant dairy conglomerate, bought up most of the land. But even though the property was now half its original size, there was still plenty of room to go around—so much so that their neighbors, the Shays, lived nearly a quarter mile away.

Josh and Winks ran around to the back and after tossing their book bags on the porch the two immediately went to work.

An entry for the Snowman's Parade was not built like your ordinary snowman. Since it had to be transported to the lake and moved several times after that, the snow had to be packed very tightly to keep from falling apart.

Most of the townspeople used the plastic mat provided by the Snowman Committee as a base and packed snow on it until it reached the desired height and width. Once done, they began sculpting a snowman out of the pile of snow. When it was completed it was tightly wrapped in blue rubber netting (also provided by the committee), the netting's clasps were clipped to the metal rings on the edges of the mat then hooked up to a snowmobile, an ATV, or some other motor vehicle and brought to the lake.

The boys worked well together and had the snow piled to the desired height within the hour. After making sure it was compressed as much as possible, they began the difficult task of actually making a snowman.

As they worked, they talked and got to know each other a little better. And it wasn't long before they realized how much they had in common.

Neither boy had any sisters or brothers and both felt uncomfortable in social situations. Both wanted to spend more time with their fathers but couldn't, and both had already made plans for the future.

"I haven't decided on exactly what I'm going to be when I grow up," Josh said as he began sculpting an arm for the snowman. "But one thing for sure, it has to involve a lot of travel."

Winks was surprised at Josh's comment. He couldn't imagine ever leaving Sparks, unless of course, his secret wish came true. He asked Josh if he was going to move away when he got older or only travel during vacations like most grown-ups did.

"I'll probably move away," Josh grunted as he finished working on the arm. "I've got posters on my wall of all the places I want to see. Australia, Hawaii, Egypt, places like that. I was thinking that maybe I'll be an airline pilot. They get to go all over the world."

"Yeah," Winks said now seeing the logic in Josh's plans. "Being an airline pilot is definitely cool."

Josh brushed some snow from his coat and picked up a trowel. "So what about you?" he asked.

Winks didn't answer right away. Instead, he pretended to be busy rounding out the lower part of the snowman. After much thought he decided to trust Josh and tell him his secret wish. Josh was cool, he figured, he would understand.

"You promise not to laugh?" Winks asked.

Josh stopped, surprised at how serious Winks had become. He placed his trowel on the ground. "I won't laugh," he replied.

"Okay," the boy said cautiously, "but remember, you promised."

Winks continued molding the snowman and kept his back to

Josh as he spoke.

"Well, you're probably going to think this is stupid, but I've always wanted to be a superhero." He waited a moment to see what Josh's response would be, hearing no laughter, he continued.

"Anyway, I always hoped that someday I'd get caught in one of those freak accidents, you know, the kind that gives you super powers."

"What type is that?" Josh asked, not sure if Winks was serious or not.

"C'mon, Josh, you know. Like when the radioactive spider bit Peter Parker and turned him into Spider-Man or like when the Gamma bomb explosion turned Bruce Banner into the Hulk. Accidents like that."

Winks finished the lower part of the snowman and placed his trowel in the snow.

"I figured I could be real good at it," he said. "Going around fighting crime, saving lives and stuff, but now…."

"But now what?"

Winks finally turned and faced him. There were tears in his eyes. He wiped his gloved hand across them and shrugged. "Well, it's just that…it's just that…now I know that it's never going to happen, that's all."

The disappointment on Winks face was so touching that Josh went over to the boy and placed a friendly arm on his shoulder. "Well hey, you never can tell," he said. "And with all the weird technology we have nowadays maybe it could still happen."

Winks shook his head. "You don't understand. In all the comic books, the guys who get super powers are already pretty brave. I mean, even if Peter Parker wasn't Spider-Man you can bet he would have stood up to a bully. And you can bet that

Wolverine of the X-Men sure would have. I just figured it out, Josh. Brave guys get super powers so they can do even more brave things. Chickens don't get anything but beat up or maybe saved by the brave guys at the last minute."

All of a sudden, it dawned on Josh what Winks was really talking about.

"You're saying this because of what happened on the bus today, aren't you?"

Winks' hands balled into fists and his face reddened with anger. "I should have punched that jerk right in the mouth and made him give me my binder back. Let him see what it feels like to be pushed around and embarrassed in front of all your friends, and I would have, I really would have but…." He dropped his hands weakly to his sides. "I…I just couldn't. All I could think of was how much it was going to hurt when Billy hit me back. So I just stood there and took it. I'm just chicken."

Josh picked up the trowel and went back to work. "You're no chicken," he said firmly. "You're ten-years-old and half the size of Billy Curtis. Now I don't read comic books much but I do know that when superheroes fight, they fight guys who are pretty much equal to them. I mean, they don't have Batman, a guy with no super powers, fighting Superman, who has like a million different powers."

"Well, actually they do," Winks replied. "In the *Dark Knight* series, Batman had this armored suit and…."

"Winks! My point is if there was a ten-year-old bullying some little kid, like a five-year-old, you would have done the same thing I did."

Winks thought about it and maybe Josh was right. If some kid was being shoved around maybe he would do something. But when he thought of facing even a ten-year-old Billy Curtis, he wasn't so sure.

"I hope I would," Winks replied as he resumed work on the snowman. "But that's the difference. You already know that you're brave. The way you stood up to him, boy, that sure was something!"

Josh waved him off. "That's different. I'm almost the same age and size as Billy and guys like him always back down from a fair fight."

Winks smiled and shook his head. "Uh-uh. Billy wasn't afraid of fighting. He fights all the time, sometimes guys even bigger than him. He was afraid of you. The way you looked him straight in the eye and stared him down. Oh, and that thing you said about him having to use a crowbar to remove your boot from the back of his head. Man! That was the coolest thing in the world."

Josh continued sculpting the snowman. "No big deal, I heard someone say it in a movie once."

Winks saw that he was making Josh uncomfortable, so he changed the topic and they talked about other things for the next half-hour or so. But there was still one thing gnawing at him. One last thing he had to say.

"Josh?"

"Yeah?"

"I don't want you to get mad at me or anything but I just want you to know that if any freak accident happens to give anybody super powers, I hope it happens to you. I think you would be a great super hero. One of the best!"

Josh didn't know how to respond. It embarrassed him yet at the same time made him feel good that Winks thought of him so highly. "Thanks," he replied and let it go at that.

It took another two hours before they could stand back and admire their finished creation.

"So, Winks, what do you think?"

Winks gave it a good going over. "I hate to say this but I think it's better than the one me and my dad built."

Josh nodded. "Yeah, it is pretty good. Now all we have to do is put on the face."

"And the hat and scarf," Winks added.

Josh put his hands to his head. "Hat and scarf! Oh nuts!"

"What's the matter?"

Josh kicked at a pile of left over snow. "I forgot about the hat and scarf. Oh, man! For two weeks my mother's been going on about me going down to the Salvation Army to pick them up. I kept saying yeah, yeah, but I never got around to it. Now, I'll bet they're all gone."

"Wow," Winks said, suddenly realizing the seriousness of the problem. "What are you going to do? You know every entry has to have a hat and scarf."

"I know."

"Do you think your parents will give you the money to buy them?"

"No. Money's real tight. Oh, man, I can just hear them now. 'If you only did what I told you and went down....'"

"To the Salvation Army blah blah blah.... Yeah, I know," Winks said. "My dad talks the same way."

The two boys sat down in the snow convinced that all their hard work was for nothing.

Suddenly Winks' eyes lit up. "Hey, I got an idea. Do you have an attic in your house?"

Josh nodded. "Yeah, why?"

"My dad keeps all kinds of stuff in our attic—old books, records, and clothes. Maybe there's a hat and scarf in yours that we can use."

Josh didn't share Winks' enthusiasm. "I don't know," he said taking off his gloves and rubbing his hands together. "My parents don't like me going up there. They say it's not insulated and the floor boards aren't sturdy."

"It'll only take a minute," Winks insisted. "We could run up, take a quick look and if we don't find anything, come back down."

Josh still wasn't crazy about the idea but dreaded the thought of having to tell his parents he forgot to go to the Salvation Army. So against his better judgment, he agreed.

"Okay," he said climbing to his feet. "But just a quick look and then we're out of there."

5

Josh turned on the attic's single overhead light and with Winks in tow, cautiously climbed the stairs. The place had an old smell and feel to it, like it belonged to another time. Boxes and crates littered the floor, pink insulation was piled into the wall slats, and plastic sheeting for the windows laid gathering dust in the corner. Although it looked well protected from the cold, Josh could see his breath every time he exhaled.

Winks was so excited at being part of this adventure that he ran up ahead and immediately opened one of the many dusty boxes.

"Cool!" he said. "There's a bunch of old books and pictures in this one."

Josh shook his head. "Forget about that. We're up here to find a hat and scarf. That's all."

"Okay, okay." Winks said with a touch of disappointment and closed the box.

They spent fifteen minutes going through crates, old suitcases, and even more boxes but the only hat they found belonged to Josh's grandfather and his parents certainly wouldn't let him use that. Convinced that they were wasting their time, Josh closed the last suitcase and signaled Winks that it was time to go.

Winks shrugged and was climbing to his feet when he accidentally brushed against something protruding from behind a pair of curtains hanging against the wall.

"Hey, what's this?" he said running his hands down the fabric and over the object.

Josh walked over and took a closer look. "What's what?"

"I think I feel a doorknob here." Winks replied. He carefully placed his hands around the object. "C'mon, feel for yourself."

Josh did and sure enough, there definitely was a doorknob there. Together they lifted up the curtains and discovered a door.

It was very old looking with chipped brown paint and glass panes that ran up and down in three separate columns. The panes were dirty and looked as if they hadn't been touched in years. But even with the dirt, both Josh and Winks could see that a room lay behind it.

"This…is…great!" Winks said enthusiastically. "We've discovered a secret room. Imagine if we were the only people who know about it?"

Josh smirked as he brushed some of the dust off his shirt. "C'mon, Winks, my grandfather built this place and my father grew up here. They have to know about the room. I just wonder why they never mentioned it to me?"

Winks seemed lost in thought. "Maybe it's a secret passageway to another universe."

Josh shook his head in disbelief. "You know, you got to stop with the comic books."

Winks put up his hands. "Okay, so it's not a door to another universe," he said hoping to avoid further comments on his choice of reading material. "Let's take a look anyway."

Josh tried the doorknob. It was locked.

"Nuts!!" Winks shouted as he spun and stomped his foot. "Now we'll never know what's in there."

Josh dug his hands into his pockets and looked around. "Wait a second," he said, "I've got an idea."

He went over to one of the boxes he had already opened, stuck his hand in, and pulled out a card from an old Rolodex file.

"Watch," he said as he approached the door, "I once saw this on some spy show. You put the card in between the doorframe and the lock like this and…." CLICK.

The boys stepped back as the door slowly opened. The hinges creaked but that only added to the excitement. What they discovered was even better then they had imagined. It wasn't just a room but a small apartment.

They entered cautiously and looked around.

There were big spots of gray on the walls where the paint had chipped off. Cobwebs laced the corners of the ceiling and the skeletal remains of some long dead field mouse lay directly in their path.

The inside had apparently been cleaned out. It was empty, with the exception of a small refrigerator, a cot, a chest of drawers, and a closet. In the adjoining room was a washbasin, toilet, and shower stall.

Winks opened the refrigerator hoping to find some ancient rotted food that would gross them both out, but that too was empty.

In the meantime, Josh rummaged through the chest of drawers but found nothing. He then tried the closet. In it were old boots, work gloves, a pair of worn out jeans, and, last but not least, a big black floppy hat and a red and brown scarf.

"Score!" Josh shouted and quickly pulled them down from the shelf.

"Talk about luck!" Winks said smiling. "That hat and scarf are perfect."

"Yeah," Josh said as he carefully inspected the items for moth holes. "They sure are. C'mon, let's get back outside and finish the snowman."

"What about this other stuff?" Winks asked.

"Forget it. We got what we came for."

Josh headed out but Winks picked up something from the floor of the closet before following him.

After leaving the apartment, they carefully closed the door and let the curtains fall back into place. As they made their way down the attic stairs, Winks asked Josh if he thought his parents might recognize either of the items.

"I don't think so," he replied. "This stuff has been locked up there probably since my grandfather's time. Nobody is going to remember that far back. Hey," he said noticing the object Winks was carrying, "what have you got there?"

Winks showed it to him. "It's an axe handle. I found it on the closet floor. I figured we could place it in the snowman's hand, kind of like a baton."

Josh nodded his agreement and, after closing the attic door, both boys ran back downstairs and out to the yard to begin putting the finishing touches on their creation.

After nearly a half hour of work, they were done.

With two pieces of coal forming the eyes, a carrot for the nose, and several black ball bearings that Josh had gotten from his father to fashion the mouth, it looked to them to be as good as any snowman they had ever seen. The hat and scarf fit perfectly and the axe handle in its right hand did seem to resemble a baton, just like Winks said it would. Overall, they were pretty impressed and were soon discussing the possibility of winning Best in Show.

Somewhere in the middle of their conversation, they noticed

that the sun had gone down and it was growing dark. Winks suddenly realized that he better get home for supper. He had been so wrapped up in the day's excitement that he forgot all about it.

"I had a great time, Josh," he said bundling up his coat. "Thanks for inviting me."

Josh smiled in surprise. "Thanks for inviting you? Winks, thanks for coming over. I never would have gotten this done by myself."

The ten-year-old fashioned a huge grin. The compliment meant a lot to him.

"When do you want to bring this down to the lake to get registered?" Winks asked as the two headed toward the road.

"How about tomorrow?"

"Tomorrow's Friday," Winks replied.

"Yeah, but there's no school until after Opening Day Ceremonies. Beside, I don't want to have to deal with Wolfman Pederuco on Saturday, everyone knows how nasty he gets with the people who bring in their entry on the last day."

"Fine with me, how we going to get it there?"

"I got a snowmobile. If my dad isn't around to help, you and I can drive it down ourselves."

That sounded a little dangerous to Winks but he nodded anyway, determined not to show the slightest sign of fear to Josh.

"What do you say afterward you come over to my house and I'll show you my stuff?" Winks said.

Josh nodded. "Yeah, sounds cool, see you then."

He waved good-bye as Winks started up the road. He continued to watch until his young friend disappeared into the night.

As Josh walked back to the house he realized that he had taken a real liking to the kid and would probably continue to hang around with him. That made him wonder whether or not he should stop calling him "Winks" and instead address him by his real name. After giving it much thought, he decided against it. Overall, he figured, Winks was a lot less cruel than Thee-o-Dore.

At six p.m., Josh's mother came home from work. Seeing her pulling into the driveway, he ran outside to help her bring in the dinner groceries.

The petit brunette wobbled on her high heels as she walked around to the side of the minivan and smiled in relief when she saw Josh coming to help her carry the packages.

As they lugged the groceries to the front door, Josh asked if she knew when his father was coming home. She replied that she didn't but assured him that his father would, as he always did, call if he was going to be delayed. Josh hoped he wouldn't be because he was dying to show them both just how well the snowman had turned out. Unfortunately, as they were putting the food away, Josh's father rang with the news that he was still at work and didn't expect to be home until well after Josh's bedtime.

Josh was disappointed but decided to use the opportunity to give his mother a sneak preview. He figured that if his mother liked it, his father probably would as well.

He led her out to the yard and flicked on the back porch lights.

As the snowman came into view, she smiled and clasped her hands in front of her face. She complimented him several times on the job he had done and walked out for a closer look. After circling the snowman several times, she expressed her amazement that two boys their size could have made something so big. Josh didn't say anything but was a little amazed himself. It certainly didn't look that big before, but he figured it probably had something to do with the lighting.

Most importantly, she didn't mention the hat, scarf, or axe handle other than to say that she thought they added to the over-all effect. Josh considered that a good sign. He felt that if she didn't recognize them, odds were his father wouldn't either.

6

Josh's father, Roy Campbell, didn't return home from work that evening until after midnight and was unaware that Josh and Winks had built the snowman.

When Winks arrived early the next day, Roy was still sound asleep. Josh wanted to wake his father so he could see what a great job they had done but Josh's mother wouldn't allow it. "Your father worked very hard to have this four day weekend and needs his rest," she told them. "You two go on ahead and bring it down to the lake. Your father can see it later."

Although disappointed, the boys nodded and went out to the yard as quietly as possible. Once there, they wrapped the snowman carefully in the rubber netting, attached it to the mat, connected the mat to the snowmobile, and set out for the lake.

AAGGGHHHHHHHH!!!!

That was the sound going through Winks' head as Josh's snowmobile pulled him and the snowman over the side streets that lead to Little Pond. Actually, Josh wasn't driving fast at all, but to Winks, who was standing on the mat with his arms wrapped around the snowman, it felt like they were teetering on the verge of warp speed.

"How you doing back there, buddy?" Josh asked.

"Fine, fine," he lied. "How much further?"

"Not far. How's the snowman holding out?"

Winks took his arms from around the snowman just long enough to give it a quick once over. "So far, so good."

Within a few minutes, they reached their destination and discovered that a large portion of Sparks' population had decided to wait until this particular Friday to register their snowmen as well.

Traffic came to a dead halt and they had to inch their way along with all the other participants down Shore Road. After what felt like centuries, they reached the entry point and eased the snowmobile down the ramp to the ice.

When they finally reached the front, they were handed a sheet of paper with the numbered location of their site and instructions on how to sign up their entry.

The directions were simple enough and the boys had no problem finding their spot. Once there, Josh parked, shut down, and glanced around at all the activity.

Workers were erecting light towers and speaker columns. Banners and flags were being strung. Trucks were bringing in supplies for the concession stands and employees of both state and private businesses were hurriedly making preparations for opening day.

"Man, this place is crazy," Josh said.

Seeing that his friend was not happy with the thought of having to deal with more lines and crowds, Winks offered to go over to the registration booth and pick up the necessary forms. Josh gratefully accepted and volunteered to unwrap and disconnect the snowman while he was gone.

Fortunately, Winks didn't have to wait in line too long and

when he returned they both sat down and started the tedious job of filling out the paperwork.

As they filled out page after page of the questionnaire, they would occasionally look up and watch the "All Terrain Vehicles" (or ATV's, as they were more commonly called) move the snowmen from place to place on the ice. Seeing all the other entries made the boys wonder where their snowman would wind up when the Opening Day Ceremonies began.

Judges usually decided an entry's final position in the Snowman's Parade sometime on Saturday. This way all the snowmen would be set up and ready when the newspapers and television crews arrived Sunday morning.

But even in this early stage Josh and Winks felt good about their creation's chances. In fact, Winks felt better about this one than the one he had built with his dad. There was something about this snowman, something special. It just seemed so big, so strong.

"This is going to win Best in Show," Winks said.

"What did you say?" Josh asked as he looked up from his paperwork.

"Uh, I...nothing," Winks replied embarrassed that he had spoken his thoughts out loud.

"Well, I'm done," Josh said putting his part of the packet together. "How about you?"

Winks replied that he was finished as well and handed his part to Josh.

"Hold the fort while I turn in these forms, all right?" Josh asked as he paper-clipped the pages together.

Winks nodded as Josh climbed out of the snowmobile and headed over toward the registration booth. With this private moment, Winks got up, went to the back of the snowmobile, and studied the snowman carefully.

"Yep! This one's a winner all right," he said beaming with pride at having had a part in its creation. Then, a sudden breeze wrapped itself around him. Winks turned, pulled up his collar, and began buttoning his coat.

"Man, I hate it when the weather changes like this," he said, putting his gloves on. Then he noticed a growing feeling of anxiety in his stomach.

He turned back to the snowman and was startled by how different it looked. Now it seemed to tower over him. And framed by the dark clouds overhead, it appeared not so much big and strong anymore, as it appeared large and menacing.

Winks shivered momentarily and stepped back. With the nervousness getting worse, and feeling like the snowman's eyes were boring into him, he quickly looked around for Josh, but was unable to find him. Thinking that perhaps he was being a little childish, he slowly turned back to the snowman in the hope that it was the shadow of the overhanging clouds that had given the snowman that ominous look. It wasn't. What Winks saw now nearly made him stop breathing altogether.

The snowman's bright orange carrot nose had deteriorated into a blackish-green stub. Around the ball bearing mouth, icicles had appeared—icicles that resembled long sharp teeth. The coal that they had used for eyes seemed to be melting, causing black rivulets to run down the snowman's "face." Winks turned away and shook his head.

Winks, calm down. Calm down, man. Don't wig out. It's just your imagination.

Taking a moment to regain his composure, he very cautiously peeked back at the snowman and was fully prepared to be up and out of there if it still looked like something out of a horror comic. It didn't, in fact, it looked exactly as it had when they arrived.

With his heart still pounding, Winks again nervously looked around for Josh and was relieved when he saw him walking back from the registration booth with the photographer. Just before Winks left to meet them, he could have sworn the snowman's eyes flashed bright red as if branding the ten-year-old for future identification.

Since it would take a while for the registration forms and photos to be processed, Josh suggested that they get something hot from the concession stands. On the way back, Winks took off his gloves and wrapped his hands around his cup of hot chocolate. "You know something?" he said as he glanced over at their creation.

"What?"

"This might sound nuts but our snowman is beginning to give me the creeps."

Josh took a sip of his hot chocolate and looked over the rim of the cup at his friend. "It's a snowman, Winks," he replied. "How can a snowman give you the creeps?"

Winks weighed his response carefully. "I don't know, it's just...Well, c'mon, doesn't it look different to you? Last night, after we finished...I thought it was by far the coolest snowman I had ever seen. I was sure it was going to win Best in Show. Shoot, even when we were coming down here, I was amazed at how good it turned out. But now, that's just what's bothering me. It seems to be changing."

"Oh man! C'mon, we're talkin' snowmen here, Thee-o-dore!"

Winks was silenced by embarrassment. For nearly half a minute he remained quiet, determined not to look anymore the fool than he already had.

It's your imagination, Winks, get a grip on yourself.

But something inside of him was demanding that he speak. Finally, when they reached the snowmobile, Winks caved in.

"Well, just look at the damn thing, Josh! I'm not nuts and I'm not some stupid kid. It's changing!"

Josh shrugged and walked over to the snowman. He gave it a good going over but found nothing unusual about it other than its size.

Josh turned to Winks. "Okay, I'll admit it does looks a *little* different, but no matter how well you build them, leaving them out overnight is going to mess them up a bit. That's why the DPW has to do daily maintenance. To keep them from getting weird looking."

Winks shook his head determinedly. "It's not just that, Josh, it's...."

Winks was interrupted by the sight of one of the committee people waving for them to come over. They waved their acknowledgment, finished the chocolate, and went over to see what the man wanted.

They were told that they were all set and that the Campbell snowman was officially registered in the Snowman's Parade. Josh thanked them, took the paperwork, and slipped it in his coat.

"I feel kind of creepy not putting your name on the registration, Winks," Josh said as the two walked back to the snowmobile.

Winks shrugged. "It doesn't matter, I don't think it likes me anyway." Feeling Josh's eyes carefully studying him, Winks finally smiled. "C'mon, let's go over to my house."

The boys climbed aboard Josh's snowmobile and took off. As they rode toward the entry ramp, Winks turned and gave the snowman one final glance.

"I'm getting to hate that friggin' thing," he muttered under his breath.

When they arrived at the Shays home, they parked the snow-mobile around back and waded through the snow to the front. Winks rooted around his pockets, pulled out the key, unlocked and swung open the big wooden door. Once inside they placed their coats and gloves on the radiator to dry.

"I'm telling you, Josh, there is just something not right about that thing," Winks said.

"Like what?"

Winks shrugged. "I can't explain it. It's just a gut feeling."

As the two sat down on the floor and pulled off their boots, Josh had a question.

"Okay, let's say there is something dangerous about the snowman. Are we talking about dangerous as in it's so big and heavy it could fall over and crush someone or are we talking about dangerous as in EVIL, you know, like Stephen King's killer car Christine or Chuckie the killer doll? Although," he said smiling, "the idea is kind of cool."

"Beware little ones!" Josh said in his best ghoulish voice. "Back to your beds, for tonight lurks Frostie the Deadman! WOOOOOO!!!"

Winks smiled at the Frostie crack but was quick to defend his position. "I can't say what's dangerous about it, I only know that it is."

Josh sniffed, took out his handkerchief, and quickly blew his nose. "Well, it doesn't look dangerous to me and your 'gut feeling' could be your nerves or your imagination."

"You don't believe in gut feelings?" Winks asked.

"Nope! AHHHHHCHOOOO! Damn! I hope I'm not getting a cold."

"Well, maybe that's because you never needed them."

"You're losing me, pal," Josh replied as they got up and walked through the hall. "You want to run that by me again?"

Winks shrugged. "It's kind of hard to explain," he replied rubbing his head. "Anyway, I can't think on an empty stomach. C'mon, let's get something to eat." Winks led Josh into the kitchen, opened the cupboard, tossed a couple of packets of cupcakes on the table, and brought over some milk and paper cups.

As they sat down, Winks continued the conversation.

"Josh, guys like you don't understand how real gut feelings are to guys like me. You've never been small or picked on. There's nothing wrong with you and nothing that makes you stick out. No one pushes you around because they know if they do, you'll push back. But it doesn't work that way for me. I've always been small. And I got this stupid droopy eyelid that makes me look sort of dopey. I swear, it's like a bully magnet. I'm always getting shoved around by people like Billy Curtis. And it would happen more often if I didn't listen to my gut feelings. It works like a warning system when things start to get weird."

Josh bit into one of the cupcakes. "So, you're saying your gut feeling is kind of an ESP thing?"

"Nahhhh, I think ESP is about telling the future. My gut feelings are more like Spider-Man's 'Spider Sense.' It warns me when I'm in danger."

Josh thought about it as he ate but still wasn't convinced. "Look Winks, I'm not trying to be a hump or anything, but your 'Spider Sense' wasn't working too good on the bus yesterday."

"Oh, but it was, Josh!!" Winks replied enthusiastically. "Just as school let out I started getting this feeling that something was wrong. I had just turned the corner when I saw Billy standing outside the bus. He was pacing and had that look he gets just before he starts in on someone. When I saw that, I ducked behind the dumpster and waited. I figured I would let him get on first, then pick a seat as far away from him as possible. Good plan, huh? The problem was that Mr. O'Hara, my math teacher, walks by and sees me. Well, before I could explain, he starts in on me with that goofball old fart way of his, 'On your way young man. No dawdling!' he says and then stands there watching until I get in line. Man, I couldn't believe it! And then, of course, I wind up ahead of Billy. And right after I take my seat, the big jerk walks by and grabs my binder. Well, you know the rest."

Josh was quiet for a moment. "That sucks, that really sucks!" he said finally. "Having to put up with that crap."

Winks reddened, he was only trying to make Josh understand that his "gut feeling" could be trusted. The last thing he wanted was for Josh to feel sorry for him. So before Josh could say anything else, Winks changed the subject.

"C'mon, let's go up to my room," he said, dumping the cupcake wrappers and empty cups in the garbage. "I got some cool stuff to show you."

Winks' bedroom was not at all like Josh had imagined. He expected wall-to-wall superhero posters. Beefy guys in spandex, posed and ready for combat with a battle cry on their lips. Instead he found it to be decorated with some superhero posters, yes, but mainly artwork covering a number of topics.

There were pictures of strange deep-sea creatures, erupting volcanoes, a holographic picture of a vase of flowers that changed colors depending on your viewing angle, and a number of unusual still photographs of sunsets, tropical islands, and the space shuttle.

"Cool," Josh said as he looked around. "Where did you get this stuff?"

"My dad's the Project Manager at Milkways. He knows a guy in their advertising department who sends them to me."

Josh nodded. "You know this poster here is really something, I must have looked at that vase of flowers at five different angles and I don't think I've seen the same colors twice. It's really pretty."

"Pra pra pra pa pa prit prit prit it it pretty pretty...."

Josh spun around to find out where the voice was coming from. "Winks, what the hec...."

"Prit prit pretty pretty ba ba ba bah bur bur bird bird. Pra pretty ba ba bird."

Josh walked over to a black covered cage hanging in the corner of the room. He lifted up the cover and looked inside.

"Winks, you got a parrot!"

Winks ran over and lowered the cover. "Shhhhhh! Don't get him started. I won't be able to shut him up."

Josh peeked under the cover again, "C'mon, Winks, let me see, you shouldn't keep a bird like this covered up all the time. It'll get sick or nuts or something."

"I wouldn't do anything like that!" Winks protested, positioning himself between Josh and the birdcage. "I leave the cover off most of the time and only put it on at night."

"Well then c'mon, let me see him."

Winks reluctantly gave in and removed the cover.

The bird was beautiful. Dark blue with feathers that were almost iridescent. Its beak was orange and its eyes the color of finely polished jade.

"Hey there, handsome," Josh said as he tapped on the cage.

"Can you say 'Pretty Bird?'"

"Oh no!" Winks said placing his hand to his forehead.

"Pra pra pra pritprit prapra pretty pretty ba ba ba bir bir bird."

Josh looked over at Winks. "You're kiddin' me right? You have a parrot that stutters?"

"Well, actually, the bird doesn't stutter, it's just that...."

"Winks, the bird stutters. I just heard it. Hey handsome, can you say, 'Polly want a cracker?'"

"Pol pol pol pol polly...."

"Holy crap! I can't believe it."

"Pol polly polly wan wan wannn wanna a cra cra cracker."

Josh burst out laughing. "Winks, this is the weirdest freaking thing I've ever seen in my life."

"It's not funny, Josh!" Winks said seriously.

"Oh, man!" Josh said. "A talking parrot that stutters!"

"He doesn't stutter, it's just that the person who taught him...."

Josh held up his hand. "I'm sorry, I'm sorry," he said trying to control his laughter. "But you can't just spring this on somebody without warning. I mean really...."

Winks tried to keep a straight face but couldn't help seeing the humor in the situation and did let a small smile peek through.

Josh rose from the bed and looked the bird over. "So anyway, what's the parrot's name?"

Winks' face immediately turned red. "I can't tell you."

Josh gave Winks a sideways glance. "What do you mean you can't tell me?"

Winks shook his head. "I'm sorry, Josh. I just can't."

"C'mon, c'mon."

"I can't!" Winks replied folding his arms in front of his chest.

Josh scrutinized his friend carefully. "You didn't goof on the poor bird and name him something like Pa paa paa pete thatha Par par parrot, did you?"

"No! I wouldn't do anything like that."

"So what's his name??!!"

Winks was silent for a moment and then finally gave in. "His name is...is...Jean-Paul Belmondo."

That did it. Josh was doubled over and laughing so hard he could barely catch his breath.

"Jean-Paul Belmondo!! Hahahahahahaha."

"It's not that funny!" Winks protested.

"Hahahahahahahahahahahaha."

"Well it's not!! Man you are so sick!" Winks said and placed the cover back on the birdcage.

Several minutes later, after Josh was laughed out, the two boys began talking again.

"I'm sorry, really Winks, but I gotta ask, how in the world did you ever get ahold of a stuttering parrot? And where did you come up with the name Jean-Paul Belmondo?"

Winks sat back down behind his computer. "Well, first of all, that's why I had the cover on Jean-Paul because I knew you'd goof on him."

"Well, I'm sorry, really. You know I'd never make fun of anyone who stutters but this is a *bird*, Winks...." Josh almost started laughing again but quickly brought himself under control. "Okay, so anyway, tell me all about him. I want to know everything."

Winks slumped back in his chair. "All right, but no more laughing. I kind of don't like my stuff being made fun of, okay?"

Josh clapped Winks on the back. "Lighten up, Winks my man. I'm not making fun of you or your stuff. And I promise not to laugh anymore unless, of course, you have a tap dancing cow locked in a closet somewhere."

Winks finally smiled. "No. No cow."

Josh sat on the bed and rested against the headboard. "Okay then, let's hear it."

7

Winks scooted his computer chair over to Josh. "Do you remember the White Birches Boarding House that used to be at the end of Mohican Street?" he asked.

Josh nodded. "Yeah, before they tore it down my dad used to deliver fuel oil there. It was run by that old lady who did the sign language."

"That's right," Winks said. "Well, there was this guy named Joe Chambers who lived at White Birches and he was Jean-Paul's original owner."

"Wait a second. You're not talking about the stuttering guy, who used to wear those heavy plaid shirts and had that wild hair?" Josh inquired.

"That's the guy!"

"I thought he was dead."

"He is. Listen, he died like a week after my mother took off, and my father saw that...well, I wasn't doing too good. So he decided that I should have a pet. A couple of days later he comes home with Jean-Paul. Boy, was I surprised! I mean, he is a beautiful bird."

"Yeah. Hey, I just figured it out," Josh said sitting up.

"Chambers lived in the boarding house that was run by that old deaf woman who couldn't read his lips because he stuttered. So he bought himself a parrot for companionship. He tried to teach the bird to talk but since he stuttered, the bird stutters. I got it!"

"Yeah, except I think it made old man Chambers really mad, you know, that the bird stutters," Winks added.

"Why do you think that?"

"Because the bird also says the F-word."

Josh had to bite down on his lip to keep from cracking up again. "The bird says the F-word?"

"Yeah, you see, I taught the bird a couple of things myself. Like he says, 'Winks my boy!' and 'Fire Phasers!' and 'Bite me.'"

"And he doesn't stutter when he says those things, right?"

"Right, because I taught him those words, not old man Chambers. But when I started teaching Jean-Paul to talk, I discovered that he learns things in groups. Like the first thing I tried to teach him was 'Winks my boy!' I must have said it to him a million times, nothing. So, I switched to 'Fire Phasers,' and said that about a million and a half times, still nothing. Finally, I got tired and said 'Bite me' every time the bird opened his beak. Well, all of a sudden the bird starts saying 'Winks my boy, fire phasers, and bite me' all at once. So, I figure the old guy must have tried 'pretty bird' and 'polly want a cracker' a million times and got nothing. So he got angry and said 'Effin' Bird!' every time the poor thing tried to speak. And well...."

"So Jean-Paul says Effin' Bird?"

Winks shook his head, "Actually the bird says 'Fuh Fuh fuh fuh....'"

Josh started to crack up again when they heard the front door open and close.

"Theodore, are you home?" asked Michael Shays.

Winks first made sure that the cover was securely over the cage before he peeked out the door to say hello to his father.

"How's it going, son?" Michael called out from the hallway.

Winks stepped just outside his room and stood at the top of the stairs. "Fine dad," he said. "I was just showing Josh some of my stuff."

"Josh Campbell?" he asked as if he wasn't sure he had heard correctly. He added his coat and gloves to the pile on the radiator.

"Yeah."

"Well, that's great! Just great!" he said enthusiastically. "Tell him to say hello to his old man for me, will you?"

"Yeah, sure."

Mike Shays nodded and headed in to the kitchen.

Winks quietly closed the door behind him. "My dad said to say hello to your dad. Boy, you would not believe how his face lit up when I told him I was hanging out with you."

Josh's brow creased. "What do you mean?"

Winks shrugged and appeared a little embarrassed. "Well, although he's never come out and said it, I think he's kind of disappointed in me. He sees you zipping around town on your snowmobile, playing hoops in the driveway with your dad. Helping him load those propane tanks on the truck, you know, being a real guy's guy and then he sees me reading a stack of comics or surfing the net and, well, I'm betting he wishes I was more like you."

Josh shook his head. "My grandfather's kind of like that with my dad. My dad's a great guy but my grandfather looks down on him because he didn't join the army right after school like he did. He thinks you're not really a man unless you've been in a war." Josh paused momentarily. "Winks, do you mind if I ask you something?"

"Like what?"

"Like how old is your dad?"

Winks sat back down at his computer desk. "He is kind of old," Winks said almost apologetically. "He was fifty-seven on his last birthday."

"Wow. But that picture of your mom over there, she doesn't look old."

Winks let out a long but quiet sigh. "She was thirty-two when she left, just took off. Didn't say a word to me. Man! I was seven-and-a-half! I still can't believe she did that!"

Winks' face began to turn red and his eyes started tearing up. Josh saw this so he got up, checked out the vase holograph one last time, then looked at his watch. "Winks, it's getting late and I want to get back to the house before my parents leave for the lake. But before I go, tell me, why did you name the parrot Jean-Paul Belmondo?"

"Why did I name him that?" Winks asked as he ran his sleeve across his eyes. "Well, the night my dad brought him home, I was up in bed trying to sleep. I heard the television downstairs and during every break they would run a commercial for this movie. I forget its name but the announcer would say 'Tonight on the Late Night Movie the blah blah blah staring JEAN-PAUL BELMONDO!!!.' It would come on like every five minutes. 'STARRING JEAN-PAUL BELMONDO!!!' It was the last thing I heard when I fell asleep so when I woke up the next day, my dad asked what I wanted to name the bird and the only thing that came into my head was Jean-Paul Belmondo."

"Definitely cool." Josh said. "But still weird."

8

Josh got home just in time to see his parents getting into the family truck. He parked the snowmobile in the garage and climbed in with them.

"Hey, guys," Josh said as he sat down in between his parents.

"Hey, son," Roy Campbell replied as he put the truck in gear and started down the road. "Your mother tells me that you and Theodore Shays built the snowman and brought it down all by yourselves. I can't wait to see it."

"Well you're going to be pretty impressed, Roy," Marion said. "Josh showed it to me last night and I have to say they did one heck of a job."

"Hmmmm," Roy nodded. "That's great. Hey, maybe you'll win Best in Show."

Josh shrugged. "Well, I don't know about that but it is pretty good."

Within minutes, they were at Shore Road. The area surrounding the Snowman's Parade was still crowded with cars but eventually they found a space and headed out on the ice to look for their entry.

Roy surveyed the lake. "There must be eighty snowmen out here. How are we going to find ours?"

"I'll find it," Josh said and took off.

Its unusually large size made it easy for Josh to pick it out among the others. The oversized black floppy hat and red and brown scarf also added to its distinguished look. He quickly ran back and got his parents.

It had been placed among several other snowmen so Roy did-n't know which one was theirs until he was almost standing in front of it. He had his arm around Josh and Marion and seemed to be in a particularly good mood. That was until Josh pointed it out and Roy got his first real look. The minute he laid eyes on it his mood changed. He pushed Josh out in front of him and glared down hard.

"What were you doing in the attic?" he demanded.

Josh's blood turned to ice water.

How did he know? How did he know?

"I uh…I mean…."

"I asked you what were you doing in the attic!!"

I'm dead I'm dead I'm dead I'm dead.

He couldn't remember ever seeing his father this angry. A hundred different excuses flashed through his head but he knew his father would see through any made up story in an instant. Lying would most certainly make matters worse. He was trapped.

"Dad look, I know you told me never to go up there, but I had forgotten all about getting the hat and scarf from the Salvation Army and I was running out of time. I just ran up, grabbed the stuff, and came down. I didn't mean to disobey you or anything, it's just that…."

"How did you get in that room?"

"I…I used one of the old Rolodex cards to jimmy the door."

"Roy, what's the matter?" Marion asked.

"Not now, Marion." Roy shot back and then turned to Josh. "Didn't I tell you that...."

Roy stopped in mid-sentence. He looked off into the distance, bit down on his lip and shook his head. "All right, Josh, what's done is done. But you listen very carefully. The minute, and I mean the very minute, the Snowman's Parade is over, I want you to take that hat and scarf and dump it in the trash. You understand? Because I never, ever want to see them again!"

"Yes, sir," Josh replied meekly.

"All right, then," Roy said, "end of discussion. C'mon, let's get out of here."

On their way back to the truck, Josh kept several paces behind his parents hoping that by laying low his father would cool down. But as they waited at the stoplight he could overhear them talking.

"Roy, what on earth has gotten you so upset?" Marion asked.

"I'll explain later," he replied, "when we're alone."

9

That night Josh found it almost impossible to sleep. He tossed and turned but couldn't seem to get comfortable.

Why did dad come down on me so hard? It wasn't as if I had set the house on fire or stole a car. Why the big fuss over a stupid hat and scarf?

He lay in bed with his eyes open, listening to the muted sounds of the television playing downstairs. In the background, he could hear the clicking sound of his father's Zippo lighter as he opened and closed it. Roy Campbell had given up smoking years ago and now, instead of reaching for a cigarette, he'd take out the lighter and snap it open and closed. It was a nervous habit and something he'd do if he was absorbed in thought or concerned about something.

Eventually the television went silent and Josh waited for the sounds of his parents climbing the stairs. It didn't come. Instead, he heard them beginning to talk. The tone was somber. He knew the conversation had to be about him. Damn, he had never seen his father so angry! No doubt, they were discussing his punishment.

Josh sat up in bed and tried to listen in, but it was no use. He could only make out bits and pieces. He didn't like the idea of sneaking out into the hall and eavesdropping but decided to risk it.

He had to know what was going on.

Quietly, he climbed out of bed and slipped through the bedroom door. He eased over to the edge of the stairway and sat down.

He could hear them clearly now and discovered, just as he had suspected, that they were talking about him.

"I should have grounded Josh for going up in that attic. Especially since I specifically told him to stay out of there," he heard his father say.

"I don't understand," Marion replied. "I know we've told him the attic was off limits but he's just a boy and you know how boys love to explore."

"I know, I know."

There was a momentary silence followed by the clicking sound of the lighter.

Roy let out a deep sigh. "Maybe I did go overboard. Josh is a good kid and I know he didn't intentionally disobey me. It's just that there are so many bad memories associated with the damned attic. And that...that room."

"You never told me about this."

Roy nodded and clicked the lighter a few more times. "I know. I should have told you when we were first married and moved in here with my father. But back then any mention of the attic would throw him into a black mood for days."

Marion placed her knitting down on the sofa. "Maybe you better tell me the whole story now."

Roy ran his hand down his face, looked at the ceiling, and tried to collect his thoughts. "You know, this is a lot harder than I thought. I mean, this is a part of my life I thought I'd never have to go through again." Roy took a deep breath and banged his flattened palm on the chair's arm. "You would not believe how much I wanted to grab that hat and scarf and burn them right there and then but...but...."

"But, if you did," Marion said. "Josh's snowman would have been disqualified."

"Yeah," Roy smirked. "Committee rules clearly state that you can't change the snowman's appearance once it's registered and photographed," he said in a singsong voice to accentuate his annoyance. "Well anyway," he sighed, his tone reverting to normal. "Since you didn't live in this town back when all this happened, I guess I'll have to start from the beginning.

"Back when I was a kid, around ten or so, this area was mostly dairy farms, this place included. The ski resorts hadn't gone up yet and the Snowman's Parade was still a local event. Milk prices were down that year, and a number of people were out of work. With the holidays just around the corner, many of them traveled from town to town taking odd jobs in exchange for room, board, and a couple of dollars on the side. A man by the name of Lucas Walks was one of those people, or so we thought. My father hired him to help out on the farm.

"I remember not liking the guy from the moment I laid eyes on him. He had greasy black hair, dark eyes, and seemed to have a permanent mad on. Always wore a big black floppy hat and scarf wherever he went. Frankly, he gave me the creeps."

"The hat and scarf Josh put on the snowman?" Marion asked.

Roy nodded. "Yep, they're his all right. Anyway, at the time there was a woman in town by the name of Martha Cleary. She was in her mid-twenties, very pretty, and owned the local bakeshop. I think she was engaged to be married, but I'm not sure. Well, whether she was or not made no difference to Walks. From the moment he saw her he began pressuring her to go out with him. She refused, but Lucas wasn't the type to take no for an answer. He started showing up at her house, calling at all hours. You get the idea. Then one day, she simply disappears. Left a note on the bakeshop door saying that she had gone on vacation and would reopen after the holidays. This struck everyone as odd because the holidays were when she did the most business. At about the same time Walks told my father that he'd been offered a job down south and had to leave right away. While he was in the attic packing his things, the police show up with a warrant for his arrest. It turns out that a couple of hunters' bloodhounds uncovered Martha's battered remains in a shallow grave up in the mountains."

"That creep!" Marion said indignantly. "But what made the police suspect Walks?"

"Just a hunch. One of the deputies remembered ticketing Lucas days earlier for a broken taillight near where Martha's body was later found. Since the area is out in the middle of nowhere and generally only used by the local hunters, the deputy decided to bring him in for questioning.

"Well, it turned out to be a smart move," Roy continued. "When they did a background check, it was discovered that Walks had been on the wrong side of the law on a number of occasions.

"He had been arrested for murder in Georgia but released when two witnesses mysteriously disappeared. And he was also wanted for questioning in Michigan. When this was discovered, the prosecutor brought in a handwriting expert to examine the note Martha supposedly left on the bakeshop door. After the analysis was completed, the expert concluded that there was a ninety-percent probability that the note was written by Walks. Unfortunately, handwriting analysis wasn't as acceptable as evidence as it is today so the judge refused to let it be entered. And since Walks' past had no bearing on the present case, that wasn't allowed to be brought up either.

"When my father learned of Walks' criminal background, it devastated him. He felt personally responsible for having brought that madman into our midst. He attended the trial every day and dragged me along with him."

"He brought a ten-year-old to a murder trial?"

"Yep. Anyway, the trial only lasted a few days and everyone was sure he'd be convicted.

"Unfortunately, all of the evidence was circumstantial. No one found a murder weapon and there were no eyewitnesses. So lacking any real proof, the jury had no choice but to find him not guilty."

Roy shook his head. "I remember people literally gasping in disbelief."

"What happened then?"

"Well, the trial was over and the jury was thanked and dismissed. The judge returned to his chambers and the courtroom began to empty out. Walks, now technically a free man, made his way over to where I sat with my father, Mike Shays, Morris Allison, Theo McKay, and a few others. He smiled at us and began to laugh."

Roy's face reddened. He pulled the lighter out of his pocket and snapped it opened and closed several times before continuing.

"When Walks finally stopped laughing, he leaned over and whispered, 'Hey guys, I know a secret. It's about that pretty little miss goody-two-shoes. Oh, that's right,' he said, placing his palms against his face in mock surprise, 'she's not so pretty anymore, is she? At least not with her face all caved in.' At that point my father began to climb out of his seat but Theo McKay held him down. Then Walks turned to Mike Shays and said, 'Mikey, Mikey,

Mikey.' He always called Mike Shays that because he knew it ticked him off. 'Mikey,' he said again, 'you seem so unhappy, and this being the holiday season and all. I know,' he said, and then this weird grin comes over his face, 'what do you say we all sing a song to lighten the mood? Let's begin with one of my favorites. It's called 'Dead Broads are a Dime a Dozen.'

"My father literally jumped out of his seat. I swear he would have ripped Walks to shreds if the bailiff hadn't dragged that lunatic away. I remember little Morris Allison trying to hold back Theo McKay and Mike Shays. It was chaos. Martha Cleary was loved by everyone and I don't think there was a person in town who didn't want to see Walks hang. But there was nothing we could do. Once acquitted, you can't be tried again for the same crime."

"So he got away scot free?"

Roy shook his head. "Not quite. But the rest of the story is a lot of old wives tales and rumor. None of it was ever proven."

"I want to hear it anyway."

"Okay, but remember what I told you. The story is that after the trial, Walks was released, but told not to leave town because the police were still looking into that matter in Michigan. Of course, that very night he jumped in his car and took off.

"Somewhere along Old Route 511, he was overtaken by a group of vigilantes and forced off the road. He tried to escape by running into the hills but his pursuers quickly caught up to him and hanged him from one of the old trees up on Thunderclap Mountain.

"Strangely enough, even in death Walks continued to be a problem. It was a very cold winter and the ground was frozen solid, so burying him was impossible. They couldn't just leave his body or try to hide it because it was hunting season and if the hunter's dogs didn't sniff him out like they had Martha Cleary, the police tracking dogs, aided with the scent from Walks' clothes, would. So, knowing that dogs aren't allowed anywhere near the Parade, they built a snowman around his body and placed it among the others. The parade runs for about three months. That's a lot of time in a murder case so tracing his killers would be very difficult if not downright impossible."

"This is unbelievable. What happened then?"

"Well, ironically, the snowman containing Walks' body was so well made that it wound up as the Lead Snowman that year. No one suspected a thing until a couple of weeks later when the snowman began to deteriorate.

"For some strange reason, the coal that was used for the eyes began to melt and run down the side of its face. The carrot rotted and turned black. Yellow and brown icicles formed on the lower part of it's 'jaw' making it look like it had a real nasty set of teeth."

"You're kidding!"

"No, really. Now, even back then they had maintenance crews. So they replaced the coal and the carrot and removed the icicles. Two weeks later the same thing happened. And again they repaired it. But this phenomenon continued until it got to the point where they were spending more time on that one snowman than they were on all the others combined. Finally the Committee decided to plow it over."

"I'll bet they got one heck of a surprise."

Roy nodded. "To say the least. But it wasn't simply the discovery of Walks' body that was so frightening. It was the way it looked. His face was a mask of pure hatred. His eyes were wide open and his teeth were clenched into this grotesque snarl. It's said that the expression was so hideous, the people from the morgue were afraid to load the body on the truck for fear it would reach out and grab them.

"Eventually, they brought out the gurney and went to collect the body. Halfway there, the ice began to crack and break up. Everyone ran back to shore and as they did, Walks' remains, frozen solid with that hideous look still on his face, fell through the broken ice, never to be seen again."

"Wow! Did they ever catch the vigilantes?"

"There was an investigation but nothing really came of it. Afterward, it was learned that Walks had become the prime suspect for that murder in Michigan. In the end, most people figured Walks got what he deserved and didn't really care who was responsible."

"If your father hated Lucas Walks so much how come his stuff is still in the attic?" Marion asked.

"Actually, the only things belonging to Lucas Walks up there were his work clothes. The day after Walks 'disappeared' my father took everything else to the landfill.

"As for the clothes themselves, do you know how some people are reluctant to touch the clothes or personal items of a person who recently died for fear of catching whatever it was that killed them? Well my father was absolutely phobic about touching Walks' work clothes for fear that some of the evil that made up the man would rub off on him. So instead, he locked the door to the attic apartment, put the curtains up, and never went up there again.

"It's funny though, ever since Pop had his stroke I've thought about throwing those things out but for some reason always put it off. Probably for the same reason my father did."

"Is that why you were so mad at Josh for going up there?"

Roy sighed. "I overreacted. Seeing that hat and scarf again made me very uncomfortable. It was like being forced back into a nightmare. I'll make it up to him tomorrow."

Just before Roy could open the lighter again, Marion gently removed it from his hand.

"I was wondering," she said. "Do you have any idea who the vigilantes were?"

"Well," he said hesitantly, "just about everybody in town has a theory but nobody knows for sure. C'mon, let's go to bed."

It wasn't until Josh heard the sound of his parents approaching that he remembered that he was still sitting at the top of the stairs. He was so caught up in the Lucas Walks story that he had forgotten that he was suppose to be in bed. He quickly slipped back into his room and slid beneath the covers.

Once his parents had closed their bedroom door behind them, Josh turned on the light. He had much to think about and it would be a long time before he would finally drift off to sleep.

10

Saturday morning Josh drove his snowmobile over to Winks' house and revved the engine just beneath his window.

After a minute or so Winks stuck his head out, knocking snow off the sill.

"Hey, Josh. What's up?" he asked rubbing the sleep from his eyes.

"C'mon out. I got something to tell you."

Winks glanced back at his clock radio. It read 7:27 a.m. "Josh, it's only…." Winks caught himself in mid-sentence. He was going to comment on how early it was when he remembered that he wasn't exactly popular in school, and if Josh, who was probably the coolest kid he knew, wanted to hang out with him at 7:30 in the morning, then hanging out at 7:30 in the morning was something he was going to do. "I mean…" Winks continued, "give me a minute to get dressed and I'll be right down."

Five minutes later Winks appeared at his front door and quietly closed it behind him. "I left a note for my dad so he won't worry. It said we were going down to the lake to check on the snowman."

"Good enough," Josh replied. "But first let's go over to the diner and get some coffee. I got some amazing stuff to tell you."

Winks nodded and climbed on the back of the snowmobile. *Coffee? Cool!* he thought.

Within minutes, they arrived at the Adirondack Diner. Josh parked the snowmobile in the parking lot and the two boys quickly made their way inside.

"Josh, I don't have any money," Winks confided.

"It's on me," Josh replied as he tossed their coats on the coat rack and hustled Winks over to one of the wooden booths.

"Josh, that's really nice, I…."

"Shhhhh, listen."

As soon as they were both seated, Josh leaned over toward Winks. "Have you ever heard the name Lucas Walks?"

"No."

The waitress came over and Josh ordered two coffees. She eyed them suspiciously, not sure if their parents would approve, especially the younger one, but the place was filling up and she didn't have time to play Mommy.

After she left, Josh continued. "Yesterday, after my old man saw the snowman, he went right through the roof! I've never seen him so mad."

"I don't understand, didn't he like it?"

"Well, you're not going to believe this but the snowman we built is wearing stuff that belonged to this guy Walks. From what I could make out he was some kind of psycho-killer."

"You mean the hat and scarf from the attic! Wow. So what else did you find out?" Winks asked.

The waitress brought over the two coffees.

"Here you go fellas. Anything else?"

"No, thank you," Josh replied and quickly took to stirring in the sugar and milk while the waitress headed off to another table.

Winks followed Josh's lead with the sugar and milk, then carefully took his first sip. WOW, it was hot! But it was also GOOD. Winks put down his cup and smacked his lips. "This is great. Soooo…" Winks said, moving his arms around in an inquisitive gesture, "tell me about Lucas Walks."

Josh told Winks what he had overheard.

Winks didn't say anything at first. Josh's description of the snowman's runny eyes, the blackened carrot stub, and the icicle fangs sounded exactly like what he had seen the previous morning when Josh had left him alone to register their entry. He was dying to tell him that he had actually seen their snowman make that transformation but was afraid Josh would think he was making it up. He could have kicked himself for that stupid comment about the attic apartment door being a gateway to another universe but he couldn't do anything about that now. He decided he would tell Josh what he had seen the snowman do after his friend had gotten to know him better and realized that he wasn't just a kid with a wild imagination.

"Well, what do you think?" Josh asked.

"Man!" Winks finally replied. "I can see why your dad was so angry." He pushed his empty coffee cup to the side and wiped his lips with a napkin. "So his body was never found, huh? That means it's still somewhere at the bottom of the lake. Hey," Winks said smiling, "remember when I told you the snowman looked dangerous? You didn't believe me. You thought I was a nut, right? Well, who's right now, Mr. Smart Guy?"

Josh smirked, picked up the check, and started digging through his pockets. "That doesn't mean anything, Winks. Just because we put a dead guy's clothes on a snowman doesn't make it dangerous.

Really. I'll bet lots of clothes from the Salvation Army are from dead guys." Josh pulled out two singles while Winks got up to grab their coats.

As they headed out the door, Winks stopped momentarily. "Do you think my dad will freak out when he sees the snowman on opening day?"

Josh thought about it for a second. "Gee, maybe he might. My dad said everyone in town was pretty ticked off about Martha Cleary's murder."

"Well," Winks said as he pushed through the door, "if he does I'll just tell him it was all your idea!"

"Thanks a lot, pal," Josh replied smiling, then picked up a handful of snow and promptly dropped it on Winks' head.

11

Nick Pederuco headed the Department of Public Works and as such was responsible for overseeing the preparations for the Snowman's Parade. Although small in size and pushing fifty, Nick was not someone you wanted as an enemy. With his jet-black hair, bushy eyebrows, and piercing eyes, he looked just as mean and short-tempered as he actually was. Generally, this was not the type of person you'd expect to see running a family-oriented event. But Nick's unwavering commitment to the parade's success, his attention to detail, and insistence on excellence made him widely respected.

But it wasn't hard work alone that built his reputation, it was his knowledge of the lake. Over the years, he studied it closely, pouring over charts, mapping currents, and checking depth markers. He learned how and when the ice formed, which places were safe, and which were not. No detail, no matter how small, escaped his watchful eye because he knew the lake's history and knew that only constant vigilance, preparedness, and foresight could keep it in check. So that Saturday morning when he walked out on the frozen surface and saw something that didn't meet with his approval he wanted answers and he wanted them now.

"Hey, Ritchie!" he shouted. "Get over here!"

Eighteen-year-old Ritchie Parker felt his stomach climb into his throat. He quickly dropped what he was doing and ran over to see what his boss wanted.

"What's the matter, Nick?" he asked, panting as he pulled up in front of him.

"You see this?" he said pointing at one of the snowmen. "What the hell is it doing up here?"

Ritchie seemed to be as surprised as his boss was. "I don't know," he replied.

Nick smirked. "You don't? Fine. Go get those other two lame-brains."

Ritchie quickly nodded and did as he was told.

With his crew assembled, Nick held out his hands toward the snowman in a "what's this?" gesture and when his three charges responded with a blank stare, he exploded.

"I want to know and I want to know NOW, who brought this snowman to the front of the parade!"

"Uhhhhhh,uhhhhh, I…errrr," the three babbled, almost in unison.

Ritchie quickly checked the tag. "It's the Campbell's. You know Josh's dad and mom and…."

Nick cut him off in mid-sentence. "I know who it belongs to, Brainiac. What I WANT to know is how it got here."

The boys hemmed and hawed but clearly had no idea.

Nick sucked in his breath and looked over his crew. "Listen to me," he said firmly. "I know you're all young and barely out of your diapers but this parade, this festival, ensures the income for the majority of families in this town. It brings people here. They spend money. We eat for another year. If it's not done EXACT-LY right, if the snowmen are not in the right positions, properly fitted in their uniforms and posed correctly with the plastic instruments, this festival will go from being the biggest winter attraction in the northeast to a statewide joke. Am I getting through to you?"

"Nick," Kyle replied, "the three of us have been working on the concession stands all morning. We have no idea how it got up here."

Nick stuffed his hands in his pockets. "Fine, fine. I guess the snowman just magically appeared here all by itself. Is that what you're telling me? Nevermind, I don't have time to fool around. Now listen, tomorrow morning the newspaper photographers and the TV people will be here and I expect everything to be ship shape and in the proper order when they arrive. Do you understand?"

The boys nodded.

"Okay, now move this snowman to its proper location and let's get this show on the road. We have a lot of work to do today."

The three boys took off.

Pederuco shook his head, checked his clipboard again to make sure everything was going according to schedule, then returned to the ice fishing shack that served as his office.

The part-time workers came on at noon and soon after things really began to take shape. Emerson & Son completed the electrical work for the overhead lights and speaker columns, and soon after Ritchie had the sound system set up and ready to go.

Kyle and Bill strung the holiday ornaments from the concession stands to the top of the speaker columns. Since the Snowman's Parade usually started in mid-December, the decorations reflected the holidays. There were Styrofoam Christmas balls, cardboard reindeer, Christmas stockings, several Menorah for the Jewish residents, and plastic horns for New Years.

Nick, as usual, growled at the last minute stragglers when they showed up with their entries. He told the registration people to process them as quickly as possible so his team could get back to work.

By late afternoon, the set up was completed and the snowmen were moved to their final positions in the parade. The crew then began outfitting them with the band jackets and plastic instruments.

When they were done, Nick looked everything over, nodded his approval, then gathered his team.

"Okay men, now pay attention. I have just been informed that the committee has selected the Skorski entry as Best in Show and as such will be the Lead Snowman. That's the one over there with the top hat and the scarf with the blue sequins. So bring that one to the front and set it up in the Lead Snowman's gear."

They did as Nick instructed. Once it was out in front, everyone agreed that it looked terrific in the neon blue band jacket and that the gold baton really added to the overall effect.

Nick then gave the okay to test the equipment. Kyle turned on the overhead spotlights and Ritchie cranked up "Silver Bells" just enough to ease everyone into the coming holiday season. The passersby ooohed and aahed at the spectacle and clapped enthusiastically to show their approval.

As the sun began to fade behind the Adirondacks, it became apparent that it would be impossible to finish it all in one day. But Nick wasn't concerned. The first few rows were completed and that's all that was necessary for the photographers. Once they were gone, he could spend the rest of the afternoon firming up the details and getting ready for the opening day ceremonies.

Nick clapped his hands a couple of times and assembled his people in front of the Skorski snowman.

"All right guys, good job. I'm proud of you," he said as the crew gathered.

"Tomorrow morning the media will be here at seven a.m. so Ritchie, I want you, Kyle, and Bill here by six-thirty. And before you clock out, make sure you get the tarps back on the snowmen. Any questions?"

His young charges were clearly not enthusiastic about having to come in so early but made no comment. Instead, they quickly covered the snowmen and headed off to the DPW garage to punch their time cards.

Unlike his crew, Nick would not be going home this evening. As supervisor, he was required to live in the shack for the first few weeks of the parade to make sure no one vandalized the equipment. Although most people might have been uncomfortable with such an arrangement, Nick was not. To him it was just part of the job. Besides, once the festival was up and running, the town would hire a security guard and he'd be off on his usual two week vacation in sunny Florida. Not a bad deal as far as he was concerned.

So, after making sure that he had left a few spotlights on to discourage troublemakers, he retired to the warmth of the shack and his portable television.

Although he was dead tired, Nick didn't sleep well that night. He twisted and turned, plagued by nightmares of being chased through the woods by an armed mob. He awoke several times in a cold sweat and it wasn't until the early hours that he was finally able to drift off to a restful sleep.

The next morning, he was rousted by someone banging on his door. Rattled by all the commotion, he climbed out of his cot, put on his coat and boots, and went to see what was going on.

"What's with all the noise!" he shouted as he yanked open the door to a wide-eyed Ritchie Parker.

Ritchie started shaking his head. "You better come out here,

Nick," he said obviously upset.

Nick zipped up his coat, pushed back his disheveled hair, and climbed out on the ice. "What time is it?"

"Ten to seven. Listen, Nick, we all got here around six-thirty like you asked and figured we'd let you sleep a little 'cause we knew you'd be up late watching over the place. We started taking the tarps off at the back so we wouldn't disturb you but when we got to the front, well, see for yourself."

Ritchie pointed to the Lead Snowman and Nick's eyes grew large. He ran over and stared, unable to believe what he was seeing.

"How...how could this happen?" he asked no one in particular. Which was just as well because not one of the boys could explain why the Skorski snowman was now nothing more than a crushed hat, a twisted scarf, and a pile of dirty snow, or why the Campbell snowman was now at the head of the parade in the Lead Snowman costume holding the gold baton defiantly in the air.

Nick stood motionless. The media people were due in a matter of minutes. The last thing on earth he wanted was their top story to be about the vandalizing of the Snowman's Parade just before opening day.

This was the first time Ritchie had ever seen Nick so utterly unable to cope. The man was like a statue, as immobile as the snowmen that surrounded him. Ritchie decided that if anything was going to be done, he'd have to do it himself.

"Nick, I got an idea," he said. "Kyle, you and Bill go to the shed, get shovels, and clean up this mess. Then we'll hook up the Campbell's snowman, drag it out of here, and put this one in front."

"Which one?" Kyle asked.

"This one here with the orange cap," Ritchie said as he quickly read the tags. "The Montgomery's. C'mon let's move!"

"It won't work," Nick said softly.

Ritchie signaled the boys to get going. "What won't work, Nick?"

Nick rubbed his hands over his face as the shock slowly began to wear off. "We can't move the Campbell snowman, look, look at the base."

Ritchie bent over and brushed some snow away from the bottom. "Oh man! Nick, the base is frozen to the ice. We'll need pick axes to pry this loose."

"I know," Nick replied still shaking his head. "And it'll take at least a half hour. We've got no choice and no time. When Kyle and Bill finish removing what's left of the Skorski's entry, leave the Campbell's where it is. Whether we like it or not, this monster here is this year's Lead Snowman."

12

That same morning during Sunday breakfast, the Campbells received a phone call. Roy picked it up and almost immediately was defending himself against accusations of involvement in the destruction of the Skorski snowman and the subsequent replacement of it with their own.

"Nick, listen to yourself," Roy replied. "Why on earth would we do anything as crazy as that? The Skorski's are friends of ours; what's more, they're my customers. No, I can't explain how our snowman mysteriously found its way to the front of the parade yesterday morning and I can't explain why it was in the front again after the Skorski's was destroyed. Look, I'm getting tired of this and I'm not going to answer anymore of your questions. Besides, where were you when this was going on? I thought you were supposed to be guarding the place. Yeah…Well, look. For the last time, I know nothing about it and another thing, Lead Snowman or not, you can keep the stupid Best in Show prize, I want nothing more to do with it."

Roy slammed down the phone and went to get the phone book.

Josh and his mother overheard the conversation and joined Roy in the living room.

"Roy, did I hear you say that someone destroyed the Skorski's snowman and put ours in its place?"

Roy nodded as he leafed through the phone book looking for the Skorski's number. "That's what Nick said, hon. Imagine the gall of that jerk suggesting that we would do something like that." Just as Roy found the number, he glanced over at Josh.

"Don't look at me, I didn't touch it, I swear!" Josh said defensively.

Roy smiled, sat down on the couch, and motioned Josh to sit down beside him. "I know you didn't, son. Believe me, the thought never even crossed my mind. But there's something else I want to talk to you about," he said, placing his arm around the boy's shoulders. "I want to apologize for the other day. You were wrong for going up in the attic but I was wrong as well for overreacting as I did. You're a good kid, Josh, and I know you didn't intentionally disobey me, so there'll be no punishment this time. We'll mark it down as a mutual mistake and chalk it up to experience. What do you say?"

"It's a deal," Josh replied and got up to get his father the phone.

Roy re-read Skorski's phone number and called their house. He was glad to hear that the Skorski family had already heard the news and assured Roy that they did not consider the Campbells responsible.

"It's sad but it seems that's the way this world is going nowadays," Lech Skorski said. "It's always a small group of troublemakers that try to ruin it for everyone else."

Roy agreed and reiterated his promise that his family wouldn't accept the Best in Show prize even if it was offered. Lech disagreed. He felt that they shouldn't allow the actions of vandals to put a damper on the festivities. The two men discussed the problem and together worked out a compromise.

Roy Campbell would accept the trophy but he would donate the thousand-dollar check to the "Hole in the Woods" camp for seriously ill children. Both men felt this was a reasonable solution and both agreed to attend the opening day festivities as a show of support.

After Roy put down the phone he pulled out his lighter and started flicking the top open and closed. "You know, this is the craziest damn thing. If I didn't know better I'd swear the lake WAS haunted."

"Haunted?" Josh replied. The boy was all ears now.

Roy smiled. "It's just an old story, Josh. You never heard about the lake being haunted?"

"No," Josh said as he sat back down next to his dad. "C'mon, tell me about it."

"Okay," Roy said putting his lighter back in his pocket. "The story begins back in the mid-seventeen hundreds. In those days, Sparks wasn't even a town. In fact, it was no more than a stopping off point between Upper New York and the Canadian Provinces.

"Back then, many of the settlers who had made the hard journey to America were becoming disillusioned by the constant warfare among the English, French, and Native Americans. Fearing more conflict, they packed up and moved north in the hope of finding a place where they could hunt and fish and raise their families in peace. Unfortunately, it didn't work out that way.

"A band of renegades, made up mostly of French, English, and Indian deserters realized that money could be made by preying upon the new settlers. They raided the camps and robbed them of their meager possessions, which they later sold on the black market. The renegades killed anyone who resisted. As time went on and their greed increased, they wiped out entire families for nothing more than a few pieces of furniture and a couple of bags of seed. When word of these attacks reached civilization, the townspeople demanded that soldiers be sent to bring those responsible to justice.

"Within days a heavily-armed brigade was sent out. They traveled for weeks carefully tracking the renegades. When the soldiers reached what we now call Sparks, the renegades ambushed them inflicting heavy causalities. But, instead of retreating, their captain ordered his men to dig in and return fire. They fought into the late evening. The renegades soon ran low on ammunition and attempted to escape by crossing Little Pond Lake.

"Now we both know that the lake is four or five feet deep for the first twenty feet or so but then drops off and becomes considerably deeper. The renegades didn't know this and weighed down with their armaments and provisions, couldn't make it across. In panic, they tried to turn back but Captain Harrison Sparks, who, I might add, is the person our little town is named after, ordered his remaining troops to block the shore and shoot anyone attempting to climb out of the water. He then told the renegades to drop their weapons into the lake and to remain exactly where they were until morning."

"So they had to stay in the lake all night? That's rough," Josh commented.

"True, but after losing most of his men in the ambush, the renegades outnumbered the soldiers and Captain Sparks wasn't about to take any chances. He figured that by leaving them standing waist deep in the lake, they couldn't escape without him hearing them sloshing through the water. And to make sure they didn't get any ideas, he had his men plant torches on the shoreline and left a few sentries on guard just in case.

"That night, as Sparks and his troops slept, the temperature dropped to well below zero. At first light, the captain and his men went down to the lake to relieve the sentries and fish the renegades out of the water. Now here is where the legend of the haunting supposedly begins," Roy continued. "In Captain Sparks' report, he stated that there had been no moon that night so his sentries were unable to see beyond the torches on the shore. And when he arrived there, he saw that the lake had frozen over during the night and that the renegades had apparently managed to escape. At least that's what he thought at first, because as he looked out on the lake, all he could see were rocks and branches strewn across its now frozen surface. It wasn't until after closer inspection that he realized that what he had thought was lake debris, was the heads, arms, and legs of the renegades. Their remains were embedded in the ice."

Josh smiled, convinced that his father was pulling his leg. "Get out of here!"

"No, I'm serious, in fact, did you know that Little Pond Lake was originally called Blood Lake? It got the name after one of Captain Sparks' men mentioned in a follow-up report that the lake had a red sheen to it when they came upon the bodies. It was the dead men's blood, of course, reflecting off the ice.

"They kept the name until after the Civil War. Then it was renamed 'Little Pond Lake,' which is much nicer." Roy looked at his son. "Do you mean to tell me that you were never taught this in school? Marion, what are they teaching these kids nowadays?"

Marion smiled. "You can't go by me, Roy," she replied. "This is the first time I've heard this story as well."

"Okay," Josh said, "but I still don't understand why they say it's haunted."

"Well, ever since that time Little Pond Lake has built up a pretty frightening history. When I was a kid, someone in my class brought in a book, I wish I could remember the name, but it was all about the strange disappearances and ghostly apparitions that have occurred there over the years."

"You can't remember the name of the book?" Josh asked disappointed.

Roy shook his head. "Sorry, Josh, but it was a long time ago. Say, why don't you take a ride down to the library? Maybe they have a copy."

Josh's thoughts immediately recalled Lucas Walks' mysterious disappearance. He was dying to know more. "Yeah, I think I will," he said.

13

Josh called Winks as soon as his parents left the living room. He told him what had happened to the Skorski snowman and his father's story about the lake being haunted.

"Man, this is sooooo cool!" Winks replied. "Just think, we have a snowman dressed in a murderer's clothes, in place of one that was mysteriously destroyed, in the center of a haunted lake. See, I told you there was something strange going on!"

Josh smiled at his friend's sense of the dramatic. "Look, my parents are dragging me to church at eleven but what do you say we meet at the library at twelve-fifteen. Tell your dad I'll drive you home on my snowmobile."

"No problem," Winks replied. "If I tell my dad I'm going to the library he'll not only drive me there, he'll pack me a lunch."

"He wants to dump the dead weight so he can watch the football games this afternoon, huh?"

"You got it," Winks replied smiling.

The two boys arrived at the library at the agreed upon time and immediately went to work at one of the computers. They hit *Title/Search* to list every book that had the keywords "Blood Lake" and "Little Pond Lake" in its description. As the little hourglass appeared on the screen, Josh blew on his hands. "Man, it's windy out there today," he said. "I can barely move my fingers."

Winks agreed. "Yeah, it's getting nasty all right. Didn't you wear gloves?"

"I did," he replied, "but the cold just seeped through. I have to buy the ones the motorcycle guys wear. You know the...."

"Hold it," Winks said. "Something's coming up."

Both boys studied the screen as it listed four books.

"Let's see, let's see," Winks blurted as he edged closer to the monitor. "Aaah, nuts. The first two are fiction. We don't want that. But the third one looks good. No, wait. It was published about thirty-five years ago. That's too old."

Josh placed his finger on the screen. "What about this one? It was only published last year."

Winks looked down and saw that the fourth listing was titled *Dark in the Forest* by Malcolm McGentry. The outline stated that it was the history of Little Pond Lake and the unusual events that had occurred there from the Blood Lake Massacre of 1756 to the present.

"Yes! Yes! Friggin' yes!" Winks said enthusiastically pumping his arm in the air. He immediately shrank down after catching a disapproving stare from the librarian. "Well, Josh," he said almost whispering, "bring it up on the screen."

Josh turned to his friend. "Bring it up on the screen? What are we, on the Starship Enterprise? If we want to read the book we're going to have to go to the book rack and get it."

"I knew that," Winks said reddening slightly.

Together the two boys went through the aisles, found McGentry's book and brought it back to one of the reading tables.

From the moment they opened the cover they knew they had hit the jackpot.

"Man, it's even got pictures!" Winks said.

"Yeah, and look at this." Josh pointed to a pen and ink sketch of a skeletal hand reaching out and grabbing the ankle of an obviously panic-stricken child. Underneath, it read, "In 1877, two respectable witnesses claimed to have seen Gunther Unis, the son of a local merchant, dragged beneath the surface of the partially frozen lake. He was never seen again."

"Cool!" Winks said as he continued to flip the pages. There were several other drawings, one more gruesome than the next, all relating to strange events surrounding Little Pond Lake. But what really caught the boy's attention was an actual photograph of the body of Lucas Walks disappearing into the icy waters amid a backdrop of snowmen.

"Check it out. Check it out!" Winks said.

"I am checking it out, just move your hand so I can see," Josh replied.

"No! No!" Winks said trying to keep his voice low. "I mean let's check the book out. I want to read it at home."

"OOOOhh," Josh replied. "Sure. Got your library card with you?"

"Library card?"

"You don't have a library card?" Josh asked teasingly.

"Well, I have a school library card."

"But no real library card?"

Winks shook his head.

"Ah, how unfortunate my little friend. You see," Josh said condescendingly as he placed his arm around Winks shoulder, "in order to avail yourself of the vast knowledge contained in these four walls it is necessary to have in your possession, a *library card.*" Winks rolled his eyes as Josh continued, "This rectangular object you see here in my hand is what I like to call my passport to adventure, knowledge, and yes, even romance. For as our forefather's once said…."

Winks pushed Josh's arm off his shoulder. "Oh, for Pete's sake, will you just have the librarian stamp the book so we can get out of here?"

Josh shrugged. "Okay."

Stopping only once at the local quickie-mart to get coffee (Winks was developing a real taste for the stuff), the boys headed directly to Josh's house. After dumping their wet clothes on the radiator, they flew up the stairs and locked themselves in Josh's room. This was Wink's first visit and he found it to be pretty much as Josh had described.

On the walls were posters of exotic places like Egypt, Africa, and the Orient and a copy of an M.C. Escher sketch. There were shelves of model airplanes and jets and although he didn't have a computer like Winks, he had a considerable library of books.

With *Dark in the Forest* in hand and determined to learn everything they could about Blood Lake and Lucas Walks, they pulled two chairs up to Josh's desk and opened the book to the last chapter. It gave a detailed accounting of the Walks trial and his subsequent demise.

Toward the end of the book, the author mentioned that he had done exhaustive research into the Walks case and concluded that Walks was hanged and his remains stuffed into a snowman by Martha Cleary's former suitor and some of his friends. The author also made note that although Walks was never convicted of any crime, the local townspeople were unusually apathetic concerning the capture of the men responsible for his death. In fact, there had been no real investigation into Walks' murder at all.

"Hmmmmm," Winks said thoughtfully. "Martha Cleary lived in Sparks and the author says he believes that Walks was killed by an enraged suitor. What's a suitor?"

"I think it means boyfriend," Josh replied. "Hey, let's start back at the beginning," Josh said. "I want to know why the lake is supposed to be haunted."

They spent nearly two hours carefully examining case histories of bizarre disappearances, drownings, and other strange occurrences. The more they read the more odd it seemed that any type of festival, let alone a family-oriented event, would be held on Little Pond Lake once you considered all the gruesome things that had occurred there.

Josh shook his head. "Wow, I never knew any of this stuff. You know, it's creepy when you think about it."

"Creepy???" Winks replied. "Man, Lucas Walks is at the bottom of the lake with a whole bunch of murdering renegades! And now our snowman is zipping around, destroying other snowmen, and getting bigger. Josh, I think it's pretty obvious that there's an entire army of zombies down there just waiting for the right time to attack!"

Winks regretted the words the second he spoke them. He had been trying so hard to be logical like Josh and now instead of acting like a trusted sidekick, he was babbling like an idiot.

Josh stared at Winks, smirked, and shook his head. "You see, that's why I hate to tell you this stuff. The first thing we have to consider is the possibility that someone real moved our snowman and flattened the Skorski's. That's who we should be looking for.

Besides, we both know there's no such thing as ghosts or zombies."

"No such thing?" Winks asked. "Wait a second. This whole book is filled with stories of ghost and zombies and people getting killed by them!"

"Stories, Winks, stories," Josh said as he placed the book down on his desk. "Look, I don't want to sound like a know-it-all but my dad told me that a lot of times regular explainable things are built up to sell books and TV shows. Take the Loch Ness monster. People still say it exists even after the navy sent down the most advanced equipment in the world to look for it. They had sensors, motion detectors, and sonar imaging machines investigating the lake for months and they found nothing. Yet people still swear that there's a monster the size of a football field swimming around down there. See what I mean?"

Winks got up and sat on Josh's bed. He was disappointed that Josh was able to easily explain away a situation he considered potentially dangerous. Josh was smart, Josh was brave, but Josh was wrong! Winks hadn't forgotten how his "gut feeling" had warned him when he was alone with the snowman and he certainly wasn't going to forget how it changed. But how could he tell this to Josh? Josh already killed his theory about the ghosts. And more than anything he didn't want to look like some scared kid.

Winks looked up and saw that his friend was watching him, waiting for a reply. He wanted to tell Josh what he thought but was afraid. Afraid of looking like a fool and losing Josh's respect. He felt his stomach tie into knots and thought that maybe he better be getting home when, out of nowhere, Billy Curtis leapt into his mind.

He remembered how frightened he was and how Josh had protected him. Josh wasn't afraid, or maybe he was but refused to show it. What if something happened to Josh because he didn't have the courage to trust his gut feeling? What if Josh died because he didn't open his mouth? Winks felt his heart sink. He was going to have to say something. Because if he didn't, the superheroes on his wall, his idols, would have to be taken down because he would be ashamed to be in the same room with them.

"You're wrong, Josh," he suddenly blurted out.

Josh looked puzzled. "Wrong about what?"

Winks steadied himself and took a deep breath. "You're wrong about the snowman. Look, I'm going to tell you something, something I should have told you before. Remember when we took the snowman down to the lake and you went over to the booth to get it registered? Remember how freaked out I was when you got back?"

Josh waved his hands. "You weren't freaked out, Winks. You just said that the snowman wasn't right and that it was giving you the creeps."

"I didn't tell you why," Winks replied.

"So, tell me now," Josh said.

Winks described what had happened and how the snowman had changed. "It looked exactly like the one Walks had been buried in, and don't tell me that I was just imagining it because I know what I saw and remember Josh, I saw it before you told me about Lucas Walks."

Winks had never felt this nervous in his life. His stomach was bouncing around like a ping-pong ball in a Lotto machine. His face was red and his hands were as clammy as a dead fish. He felt like he had just gone ten rounds with Billy. But he didn't regret it, not one bit. The superheroes would be proud of him.

"How come I didn't see it?" Josh asked.

"I don't know."

"Yeah, well, if I saw that, I would have been scared too," Josh replied.

Winks eyes brightened. "You mean you believe me?"

Josh hesitated before responding. "I don't know what to believe, Winks," he said. "But I was thinking about what you said about gut feelings. Maybe you are more sensitive to this kind of stuff. So just to be on the safe side, maybe we'd better consider all the possibilities."

Winks felt like a huge weight had been lifted off him. His stomach settled down and his hands and face returned to normal. "Are you going to Opening Day Ceremonies tomorrow?" he asked.

Josh stood up from his chair and stretched. "You kidding? Everyone goes to Opening Day Ceremonies. We're even bringing my grandfather from the nursing home with us."

"Yeah, I remember my father saying that he had had a stroke. How's he doing?"

Josh shrugged. "Not bad. In fact, he's walking with a cane now."

"Okay then. Tomorrow we meet at the lake and give the snowman a good going over."

"Not tomorrow, Winks," Josh replied flopping back in the chair. "Since I don't get to see my grandfather that much I'm sure my parents are going to want us to spend the whole day together as a family. You know what I mean."

Winks nodded. "Yeah, my dad's like that too. So, after school Tuesday?"

"Sure."

14

The Opening Day Ceremonies for the Snowman's Parade began promptly at ten a.m., yet by eight-thirty, hundreds of people had already gathered around the lake, braving the cold just so they could be among the first on the ice when the festivities began.

The skies were clear and blue and filled with wispy winter clouds. Pine-scented winds blew in from the west. Music played in the background and the smell of buttered popcorn, hot chocolate, and fried dough filled the air. The motels were almost completely filled and restaurants were doing a brisk business. From the looks of things, it was going to be another banner year for the town and many of the locals had gathered at the ice shack to congratulate Nick Pederuco and his crew for a job well done.

When the library clock struck ten, trumpets sounded, balloons were released, and people began filing out onto the ice to look at the snowmen and participate in the numerous scheduled activities. There were outhouse races, iceboat exhibitions, snowmobile shows, and synchronized skating. For the finale, a fireworks display was scheduled along with the awarding of the Best in Show prize.

Since this was Grandpa Ernie's first family outing since recovering from his stroke, the Campbells were in no hurry to battle the crowds and decided to wait until noon before picking him up at the nursing home.

When they arrived, the elder Campbell met them in the lobby and gave them all a big hello. Although still big and imposing, Roy noticed that his father had lost a little weight, and that his hair was a shade whiter than it had been. But overall, he looked well on the road to recovery. They exchanged hugs and kisses and small talk for a while, then climbed in the minivan and set out for the lake.

Attending the Opening Day Ceremonies was a tradition for the Campbells, not only because they always participated in the Snowman's Parade contest but because it gave them the opportunity to meet up with old friends and swap stories with visitors from other parts of the country. It was something they all enjoyed and looked forward to. Unfortunately, this year, the specter of Lucas Walks had dampened Roy's enthusiasm. He knew the second his father saw the hat and scarf on the family snowman there'd be trouble.

Roy spent days planning how he would handle it. Taking into account his father's shaky health and volatile temperament, he decided that when asked (and this was definitely a "when" not an "if" situation), he would simply remind the old man that Walks had been dead for thirty years and that the Snowman's Parade provided the perfect opportunity to get that stuff out of the attic once and for all.

He hoped that such a casual attitude would keep his father from overreacting. Unfortunately, logic and reasoning were not his father's strong points. There would no doubt be some kind of confrontation but hopefully it would blow over quickly. If not, well, he'd cross that bridge when he got to it.

As they drove down Shore Road and circled around for what

seemed to be forever, a parking space finally opened up and the Campbells set out to join the festivities.

Roy's concerns about his father's health turned out to be unfounded. Ernie needed no help getting out of the car and with the aid of a sturdy cane easily kept pace with the rest of the family. He shrugged off Roy and Marion's numerous attempts to assist him, but graciously accepted Josh's offer to take his arm for extra support.

When they reached the lake, Nick escorted them to the front of the line. Roy wasn't particularly happy that his family was being singled out for special treatment but nodded his thanks and acceptance of Nick's obvious peace offering.

As they approached the parade, Roy was relieved to see the Lead Snowman was surrounded by tourists. Using the crowds as an excuse, he suggested they start at the back and work their way forward. The family agreed and they spent the next half hour looking over the snowmen, chatting with neighbors, and occasionally gazing out at the sport competitions being held off the east shore. As in all pleasant gatherings, time passed quickly and they soon found themselves nearing the front of the parade and Shore Road.

Seeing that the crowds were still blocking the Lead Snowman, Roy quickly came up alongside his father and began talking about the difficulties he was having with his new business in an attempt to maneuver the old man past it. Ernie listened attentively and was about to comment when, suddenly, a gap in the crowd opened up and Ernie caught his first glimpse of the snowman. He immediately broke ranks and walked over to get a closer look. With Josh at his arm and his family in tow, he brushed past the crowd, stepped up to it and studied it carefully. "Roy!" he thundered. "Is this what I think it is?"

Roy joined his father and sighed. "If you're asking if these are the clothes from the attic, the answer's yes. Look dad, that stuff's been laying up there for thirty years. It was time we got rid of it."

Ernie Campbell's face tightened up. "Got rid of it? Damn it, boy, you should have burned it! I should have burned it thirty years ago and sent it straight to hell so Lucas could have somethin' to wear while he rots down there!"

Roy replaced Josh at his father's arm. "Now now, dad, calm down. Walks has been gone a long time and these are only old clothes. Nothing more. Don't get yourself upset. You don't want to get sick again."

"Oh, get your hands off me!" Ernie said shrugging him loose. It was then that he realized where he was standing and what position the Campbell snowman held. "Good Lord," he said quietly. "This is the Lead Snowman!" Josh looked up, surprised by the look of fear in his grandfather's face. "The Lead Snowman," the old man said again.

Roy put his hand on his father's shoulder. "So what if it is, dad?" Roy said calmly. "That doesn't mean anything. Look, you're getting tired. Let's go over to the concessions and get a bite to eat."

Ernie was about to say something, thought better of it, and then walked away leaving his son behind.

Due to the cold and the fact that Ernie had become sullen and withdrawn, the family decided to pass on the outdoor concessions and walk down Main Street to one of the restaurants. Although crowded, they didn't have to wait long and were soon ushered into the dining room and seated next to the stone hearth.

Welcomed by the warmth and the smell of good food they quickly scanned the menu and ordered, with grandpa insisting on cocktails for the adults.

The food was good and the cold weather made for a healthy appetite. They ate quickly and, with the help of two bourbons,

Ernie regained his normal pallor. But there was no mistaking the fact that the sight of Walks' old clothes was still gnawing at him.

"It's my own damn fault," the elder Campbell said as he pushed his empty plate to the side, "I must have been crazy to leave those things lying around up there."

"C'mon, dad, let it go," Roy replied taking a sip from his drink, "besides, Josh is going to dump that junk in the nearest trash can as soon as the festival is over."

Ernie vigorously shook his head. "Ain't good enough just to dump it. You got to burn it. Burn it the way you burn anythin' that's infected and diseased. And boy," he said turning toward Josh, "you keep away from that damn snowman."

Roy put his drink down just loud enough to get the old man's attention. "Dad," he said firmly, "we're trying to enjoy lunch and the fact that we're all together as a family again. With your therapy and me working the hours I do, we don't get to do this as often as we should. So let's just forget about Lucas Wal...."

"Josh," Ernie said interrupting his son, "You know anything about Lucas Walks?"

"Well, Grandpa," Josh said, carefully measuring his reply, "I got a book that tells all about him. It even has a picture of his body as it slipped into the lake."

"Where in blue blazes did you get something like that?" Roy asked incredulously.

Josh stiffened a little. "Me and Winks went to the library to look up the history of Little Pond Lake. To see why it was haunted. Remember? You told me that some kid in your class...."

Roy backed off. "That's right, I remember," he said. "I just don't recall anything about Lucas Walks being in it."

"Well, Roy," Marion said. "I'm sure they must have updated

it since you were in school."

Roy nodded. He was hoping for the chance to interject a new topic but try as he may, he couldn't get a word in edgewise. Once the elder Campbell started talking there seemed to be no stopping him.

"Damn lake is haunted, boy," Ernie told Josh, his voice booming over the din of the restaurant. "When I was a lad we all knew it and were mindful to show it respect. Nowadays, with all this science and computers and crap people forget some of the old wisdom. You know, just because you can't prove somethin', doesn't mean it ain't true.

"So listen to your old grandpa and remember what I tell you. When you're out on that lake keep your eyes open and your wits about you."

"Oh, dad, really," Roy said, rolling his eyes. "The lake isn't haunted. Sure, there have been accidents over the years but you make it sound like Jaws is swimming around down there for heaven sake."

Ernie smirked condescendingly, shook his head, and then turned back to his grandson. "Now listen to me, Josh," Ernie continued, his eyes dark and penetrating, "no book, no matter how well written, can tell about an event better than being there your own self. And I was there. I knew Lucas. I worked with him, ate with him, and paid him for his labors. And just like everyone else in this town, I was fooled by him. And I'm telling you boy, he wasn't just a man gone bad. He was a man in league with the devil. And I promise you, on Judgment Day, when the good Lord asks me about my dealings with that monster, I'll tell Him to His face that Lucas Walks was the evilest bastard who ever walked God's green earth."

"Dad!!" Marion said casting an eye at Josh.

"Oh, sorry," Ernie replied with a slight smile. "Pardon my French, boy."

"Can't we talk about something else?" Roy asked hoping finally to put an end to the conversation.

"Oh hell," Ernie said wiping his hands on the napkin. "What else is there to talk about? You got Lucas' clothes on that snowman of yours. Appears he's the man of the hour."

Roy shook his head and excused himself to go to the bathroom. Marion, on the other hand, had been waved over by one of her friends from the church group. She too excused herself but promised to return shortly.

"Looks like it's just you and me, Josh," the elder Campbell said as he motioned to the waitress for a refill.

With his dad gone and his mother at another table, Josh saw an opportunity to question his grandfather about the legendary Lucas Walks.

"Grandpa, in the book it says that Lucas was murdered by some of the local townsfolk. But there was no investigation. How come?"

Ernie sucked his teeth and considered his answer. "No evidence," he said finally. "Remember, Lucas was dead over a month before they found his body. There were no witnesses, no murder weapon, no nothin'. Who were they gonna charge with the crime?"

When the waitress returned with his drink, he winked at her and slipped her a five-dollar bill.

Josh had the feeling his grandfather was evading the question and decided to press him a little further. "But," he continued, "the book says he was murdered by an enraged suitor. They must have had somebody in mind."

Ernie sat up, clearly not liking the way the conversation was going. "Now look, son," he said, "like I said, there was no evidence. Nobody was charged with anythin'. But to answer your question. Lucas was killed all right. He sure as shootin' didn't die of no heart attack!" At this the old man laughed and showed his pearly false teeth. "Yep, no doubt about it. He was killed but he wasn't murdered. Only innocent people are murdered." The old man then belched and wiped his mouth with his hand. "You see, people like Walks are like rabid dogs. The sooner you put them down the better. Back in my day a man did what had to be done. If he made a mistake he did whatever he had to do to make it right."

There was something in the tone of the old man's voice that sent a shiver up the boy's spine and he anxiously began looking around, hoping for his parents return and a change of topic.

The old man's face began to redden as the liquor took hold. He smacked his lips and turned toward Josh again.

"Responsibility! That's the key," the old man said. Josh looked at his grandfather and saw a coldness in him that he had never seen before. Suddenly the old man took a deep breath and pounded his fist on the table. "That damn snowman is an abomination!" he thundered. Then he turned back to Josh, his reddened eyes betraying dark secrets. "It must...be...destroyed."

Fortunately, it was then Roy exited the restroom and returned to the table. "So, how's it going you two?" he asked as he sat back down.

"Fine, dad," Josh said maybe a little too enthusiastically.

"Well, that's good," Roy replied as he looked around for Marion. When he spotted her he gave a little head signal indicating that it was time for them to be on their way.

After they paid the bill, Marion went over to say good-bye to her friends and Josh went to get their coats. While they were gone, Roy studied his father carefully.

"You know, dad," he said, "you really shouldn't be drinking. You still haven't fully recovered from your stroke."

"Oh leave me be, you old mother hen," Ernie snapped. "A

little ol' Pete never hurt anybody, besides, I do believe it's cleared my head some."

Roy let it go. "All right fine. Listen, I have some business to attend to. What say you, Marion, and Josh go on back home. I'll catch a ride and meet you there later."

"Sounds fine by me," the elder Campbell replied smiling.

Later that evening, Roy returned home with the Best in Show statuette and, before joining his family, quietly placed it on the floor of the closet under the stairs. He saw no need to wave it under his father's nose and get him all fired up again.

The family was seated in the living room when Roy entered and took his chair.

"So, how's everyone doing?" he asked.

"Fine," Josh replied as he poked at the embers in the wood stove.

Roy sniffed a couple of times. "Ummm, something smells good," he said inhaling the aroma of freshly baked dough.

"That would be Marion's cooking!" Ernie boomed. "Best pastries I've had in nearly a year."

Marion blushed pridefully. "Oh, dad."

The rest of the evening passed uneventfully. They had seconds on desert, more coffee (with Ernie sneaking a shot of bourbon from Roy's liquor cabinet whenever the opportunity presented itself), played some cards, and discussed plans for Ernie's return home once his therapy was completed.

The Snowman's Parade was not mentioned nor was Lucas Walks for the rest of the evening. This delighted Roy and convinced him that his plan for playing down the sudden return of Walks into their lives had been a success.

"Well," Ernie said climbing out of his chair. "It's time I was on my way. Roy, call me a cab, will you?"

Marion looked at Roy, puzzled by the old man's request. "Cab? Dad, if you want to go, Roy will gladly drive you home."

Roy got out of his chair but Ernie raised his hands. "Now, listen to me all of you. The time has come for you to stop thinkin' of me as some old cripple. My therapist says I'm almost back to where I was before the stroke, so you can stop treating me like a child. Now, Roy, are you going to call that cab or am I going to have to do it myself?"

Roy, not wanting to put a damper on what had been a pleasant evening, capitulated. "Fine, dad, fine," he said defensively. He walked over to the phone and made the call. After giving their location and destination, Roy announced that the taxi would be there in ten minutes.

"Well then, I'd better get my coat," Ernie said smiling. "It'll take me that long just to walk out to the curb."

Roy and Marion again tried to persuade him to let them drive him home but he made it clear that his mind was made up thank you very much.

With Roy and Josh on either side of Ernie, they slowly walked down the snowy path to the street. The taxi arrived promptly and the family said their good-byes. Roy hugged his father and Marion kissed him on the cheek. Josh being at that awkward age didn't know whether to hug him, shake his hand, or kiss him. The old man solved that problem by grabbing the boy and pulling him up close for a hug.

"You remember what I told you, Josh," he whispered. "Responsibility."

Josh nodded and gave his grandfather one last squeeze. The old man then smiled, let him go, and climbed into the cab. As they waved good-bye, Josh had this bizarre tingling sensation in his stomach. For some reason, he immediately thought of Winks.

Gut feeling?

As they walked toward the house, Josh continued watching the cab until its tail lights faded from view.

15

Ernie looked out the back window and watched as his family walked up the path toward the house. As the cab made its way down the road, he informed the driver that they would be making a detour before heading to the nursing home.

"Can't do it, pal," the driver replied. "With the Opening Day Ceremonies, everyone's liquored up and calling for rides. I got two fares waiting. Besides, the festivities are over. Everyone's gone home."

"Fine then," the old man said. "Forget the nursing home, just take me to the lake. I'll get another cab there."

The driver turned around for a second. "Are you kidding? You were lucky to get me. You're not going to find another cab...."

"I said take me to the lake!" Ernie said firmly as he leaned up behind the driver's head. "And when I need your two cents, I'll ask for it."

"Fine, Pops, you're the boss," the driver replied, but not before giving Ernie a look that indicated that he thought the old man was out of his mind.

Frankly, Ernie didn't care what the driver thought. He had

something to take care of and by heaven, he was going to take care of it.

When they reached Shore Road, the cab driver made the turn toward the lake and brought the vehicle to a stop in front of the Snowman's Parade.

"Good enough?" the driver asked sarcastically.

Ernie didn't reply. Instead, he quickly scanned the area for any sign of life. Seeing no one, he turned his attention to the ice shack. It was dark.

After the driver read him the fare, Ernie climbed out of the cab and closed the door with his cane. He reached into the window, gave the driver the money along with a generous tip, tapped the roof, and sent him on his way. As the cab disappeared up Shore Road, the old man turned toward the lake and steeled himself for the job ahead.

Again scouting the area to make sure he was alone, Ernie walked past the concession stands and ticket booths and cautiously eased himself onto the ice. Although his eyesight wasn't as good as it had been before the stroke, he could still make out the snowmen figures in the distance as they glistened under the few soft lights.

His plan was to grab the hat and scarf and set fire to them in the nearest trashcan. No big deal. No real harm done. People would most likely blame the tourists. It wouldn't be the first time someone walked off with souvenirs. Besides, all the news stories and photos had already been run. Within days, the hat and scarf would be forgotten and the entire matter put to rest.

Such thoughts strengthened the old man's resolve. He bundled his coat and continued his journey.

The sound of the snow crystals crunching under his feet and the cold crisp air brought back memories of a night very similar to this one. A night long ago when he and his friends brought down a serial killer, packed his body inside a snowman, and dragged it out on the lake.

He stopped for a moment to catch his breath, rested his cane between his legs, and adjusted his muffler and gloves. Surely, he should have reached the parade by now. It certainly didn't seem this far when he started out. Yet somehow, there they were, still several yards in the distance. Determined, he pressed forward toward the dark silhouettes.

Try as he might he couldn't make out the form of the Lead Snowman.

Where the hell is it?

Spurred by curiosity, he walked faster until he reached the front of the parade and discovered that the Lead Snowman simply wasn't there. Bewildered, yet determined not to have to do this again at some later date, he began scouring the area. A few rows back he saw what he thought was his family's entry tucked in among the others. He hobbled over only to discover that it looked nothing like the Lead Snowman. In fact, it was a dwarfish creation with reddish pits surrounding the "face" that seemed to resemble pockmarks. Cursing his own frailties, he swore to check each and every snowman if necessary until he found the one he was looking for.

As he walked along the rows, he was surprised at how ugly the snowmen looked under the pale light of the moon. It fact, they didn't even look like the same snowmen he saw earlier that day. He came across several others that appeared to be pockmarked. One had an eye patch, one a crutch, and several more were missing pieces of coal around the mouth area so it looked as if they had lost teeth.

Damnedest thing.

He was nearly fifteen minutes into his search when he began to feel disoriented and a little dizzy. Were the lights dimming? Why did it seem so dark?

He looked around, yet couldn't seem to find a point of reference. He wasn't even sure if he was heading toward the back of the parade or toward the front. He knew that all the snowmen should be facing Shore Road but as he walked in that direction, it seemed that Thunderclap Mountain was getting closer, which was impossible; Thunderclap Mountain was on the opposite side of the lake.

Although Ernie was as determined as ever, this obviously wasn't working out.

Accepting his failure, he turned in the direction he believed to be Shore Road. He was about to take his first step when he spotted the snowman, large as life, standing in the middle of the lake. At first, he thought it odd that the maintenance crew would move it so far from the others but remembered that restoration work was always done in the early morning and away from the eyes of the public.

Invigorated that he had not come this far in vain, Ernie confidently approached his target.

"Well, well, my frozen friend," he said as he hobbled nearer. "Looks like you and I have a little business to tend to."

Out of nowhere the wind swept across the ice. The cold sent needles into his aged hands and he began having trouble holding onto the cane. He winced as the icy mist stabbed at his face and he felt his false teeth loosening in his mouth. He again considered giving up but the sight of the snowman's grinning countenance with Walks' hat perched on its head stirred something within him. It was as if Walks was once again tempting him, daring him, challenging him to come ahead and take his best shot.

Well, then, that's what he would do.

Ernie, now finally face to face with the snowman, grinned and reached up to remove the old black hat. Again, the wind picked up. Slowly the snowman's scarf seemed to come alive. It rose from its shoulders and weaved in front of him like a cobra. Puzzled, the old man lowered his hand. Suddenly, the scarf lashed out and like a wet rag slapped the old man across the face. Furious, he raised his cane and swung at it.

The sudden motion threw him off balance. He began to wobble and had to place his free hand against the snowman to keep from falling. As he attempted to get the cane back under him, the scarf slowly snaked up from behind and loosely wrapped itself around his throat.

Once he had steadied himself, he took a deep breath and felt the bundling around his neck. Believing that his own scarf had become tangled, he reached up.

The scarf abruptly pulled tight.

Ernie's false teeth catapulted from his mouth, fell to the ice, and shattered. The cane clattered to the surface beside them as he struggled to break free. He pulled frantically but the scarf continued to wind itself around his throat like a boa constrictor. In desperation, he threw himself backward hoping to yank the snowman's head off but it wouldn't budge.

Now red faced and out of air, he kicked at the white behemoth. Seeing it had no effect he tried again, only this time he tripped over the cane and his legs fell out from under him.

As the surface rapidly approached, he instinctively put out his hands to protect his face. Just before he struck the ice, the scarf, still tightly coiled around his throat, pulled taut and yanked his head backward. He heard a terrible snapping sound and darkness quickly closed in from all sides. With his last breath he gazed at the snowman and saw the shadow of a face he had last seen thirty years ago.

"Walks!" he whispered, then fell dead.

16

The following morning the front door bell rang and Roy wondered just who would be calling so early.

Curious, he listened as Marion padded out and opened the door. There was some conversation and Roy overheard what was clearly a man's voice. Although he couldn't make out the words, the tone sounded official, somber. Was something wrong? Could his father...? He tried to dismiss that thought as absurd, but there was an undeniable ring of truth to it. It was like searching for a canker sore with your tongue. You move it around from place to place and it isn't until you feel the pain of contact that you know your search is over.

"Roy?" Marion said entering the room. "Sheriff Parker is here. He says he needs to speak to you right away."

With what felt like a swarm of eels writhing in his stomach, Roy Campbell nodded and slowly walked out to the hallway to meet with a grim-faced Sheriff Alvin Parker.

The sheriff looked up. "Roy," he said, "I have some bad news."

"Is it about my father?" he asked, hoping the answer would be no.

The sheriff nodded his head solemnly.

"Oh, Lord," Roy said quietly and sat down on the hallway steps.

"I'm sorry," the sheriff replied. "He was found dead on the lake early this morning. There was nothing anyone could do."

"The lake??" Roy asked, startled.

"Hey, what's going on?" Josh asked from the top of the stairs.

Sheriff Parker saw himself center stage in what was clearly a family matter and suggested he and Roy go out to his patrol car to continue the conversation. Roy, sensing that the details surrounding his father's death might be a little too upsetting for Josh, agreed.

Once inside the car the sheriff opened his notebook and revealed the circumstances of Ernie Campbell's passing.

"Nick Pederuco called me at five a.m.," Alvin began. "Said he had gone outside to check on the propane tank and saw that the Lead Snowman wasn't where it was supposed to be. According to him, that's been happening a lot lately. Then he told me that he began checking the rows and had gotten all the way to the back when he saw that someone had moved your snowman to the middle of the lake. Nick says this really ticked him off so he went out there and, as he got closer, saw your father's body. Now, Roy, brace yourself because this is the hard part. Somehow, the snowman's scarf got tangled around your father's throat. Maybe one of the tassels snagged a button or something, I'm not sure. But from what I could see, it looks like he lost his balance and as he fell, the scarf went taut, breaking his neck.

The sheriff pursed his lips and shook his head. "What got me was why the scarf didn't pull the snowman's head off, you know, with the weight of your father, but Pederuco said that some people insert a large icicle from top to base to strengthen it for the ride to the lake. You ever hear of that?"

"Yeah, I have. In fact I taught my son how to do it."

Alvin nodded and began writing in his notebook.

Roy pressed his hands to his forehead. How could his father have died at the lake? It didn't make any sense. He put his father into a cab himself and watched as it headed off toward the nursing home, so how could he have...? He suddenly remembered that it was his father who had insisted on the taxi in the first place.

Had he been planning to sneak down to the lake all along? But why?

It didn't take long for him to answer his own question. Roy momentarily closed his eyes.

Oh, dad, why couldn't you have simply left it alone? It was only a stupid hat and scarf. It wasn't that important.

Sheriff Parker looked up and took a deep breath. "I'm sorry, Roy. Apparently, it was just a freak accident. There's no sign of foul play."

Roy nodded and reached for the door handle when one of the Sheriff's earlier comments echoed back at him. "Wait, wait. How did the snowman get to the middle of the lake?"

"Pederuco says he has no idea," Alvin replied. "According to him, it was still at the front of the parade when he turned in for the night. And there is something else. Nick says the DPW hadn't plowed that far out because of Opening Day Ceremonies, so that light dusting of snow from the other night was still fresh. When I walked out there, I noticed that there were no mat tracks, tire tracks, or sled tracks leading to the snowman. Just one pair of footprints. Your father's."

"But you said Nick went out there."

Alvin nodded. "Yes, but only so far. I could see the exact point where Nick discovered the body and ran to the phone to call me."

The shock was beginning to wear off and Roy suddenly realized that he would never see his father again. Tears welled up in his eyes and he fought to hold them back.

The sheriff, having had the unhappy duty of bringing tragic news many times in his career, saw this and closed his notebook. He wanted to ask Roy if he knew why his father had gone down to the lake but saw that this was neither the time nor place. Instead, he quickly explained the procedure of identifying the remains and having a funeral home tend to the body.

"I'll make the arrangements right away," Roy said opening the car door. "Alvin, I know this isn't easy for you. I appreciate your coming by and telling me personally."

Alvin nodded.

Sheriff Parker left the Campbell's and drove back to the parade. The fact that there were no tracks to explain how the snowman got to where it was still haunted him. If there was only someone who had seen what had happened.

What the sheriff didn't know was that there was such a person. But that person had a long history of keeping secrets.

17

In school that same morning, Winks was scouring the hallways for Josh so they could get their investigation plans firmed up. Because of the difference in their ages, they shared no classes but Winks expected to bump into him at least once during recess. He didn't realize that anything was wrong until he stopped one of Josh's teachers in the hall.

"I'm afraid there's been a death in Josh's family," Mr. Wilkins told Winks. "Apparently his grandfather passed away last night."

A million questions came to mind yet Winks couldn't give voice to any one of them. He just stood there slack-jawed staring at Mr. Wilkins. Finally, the bell rang and the teacher nodded, turned, and walked off leaving Winks standing alone.

Yesterday, Winks had attended the Opening Day Ceremonies with his father. And like the Campbells, arrived around noon. Seeing that the Lead Snowman was surrounded by people having their pictures taken, Mike and Winks decided that they'd come back and see it later.

They wandered through the rows admiring the snowmen, watched the snowmobile races on the east shore, and chatted with neighbors and friends.

While walking around, Winks spotted Josh and his grandfather a few times and was sorely tempted to call out and say hello. But after some thought decided against it. Josh had made it clear that he was going to spend the day with his family and since Winks didn't want to appear intrusive, he stayed away.

The Shays entry made it to the fifth row, which was pretty good considering how much competition they were up against. Only the most attractive snowmen made it to the front.

As the day progressed, Winks and his dad talked and joked and made plans for a late lunch in town. Everything was going fine until Mike Shays decided he wanted to see the Lead Snowman before they left.

The area surrounding it was still swarming with people but Mike took Winks by the arm and squeezed through the revelers. He saw the neon blue band jacket and gold baton first and was impressed with how big it was. He was just about to comment on what a fine job the boys had done when he suddenly recognized the hat and scarf.

Suddenly, his eyes narrowed and his lips became a thin white line. His face grew dark and cold. He looked down at his son and demanded to know where the items had come from.

Winks' "gut feeling" immediately kicked into high gear and after remembering Josh's dad's reaction, Winks scrambled to play it down. He "matter-of-factly" shrugged and told his father that they had found them while rummaging around Josh's attic. They can't be very important, Winks added, because Josh's dad had told them to dump the clothes in a trash basket right after the parade season was over.

Mike Shays eyed his son carefully while mulling over Winks'

explanation. He then nodded and after a few minutes regained his normal composure.

They ate and the rest of the day passed uneventfully. Nothing more was said about the hat and scarf. But throughout the day Winks' "gut feeling" continued to nag him, telling him that something was terribly wrong and that time was running out.

That was yesterday. Today Josh's grandfather was dead.

18

When Ernie Campbell's obituary appeared in the *Adirondack Times*, it stated that he was a resident of the Sparks Community Care Center and was recovering from a recent stroke. It went on to say that he had been a lifelong resident of the town and had unfortunately passed away after attending the Opening Day Ceremonies with his family. Nowhere in the paper was there any mention of the mysterious circumstances under which he died.

In Sparks, however, omitting such unsettling facts wasn't unusual. No one, including the newspapers, wanted anything to interfere with the success of the parade. So Ernie Campbell's death was played down as nothing more than the untimely passing of a well-respected, yet old and feeble, local resident.

Morris Allison scanned the obituary and tossed the newspaper to the floor. He didn't need to be told about Ernie's death. He had seen the entire thing with his own eyes.

Morris was forty-nine years old, stood only five-feet six-inches tall, and couldn't have weighed more than one-hundred and thirty-five pounds soaking wet. He had long gray hair, a stubble beard, a drinking problem, and a reputation as a reclusive oddball.

He was also a very wealthy man.

The Allison estate stood majestically overlooking the west bank of Little Pond Lake. A virtual palace, it consisted of fifteen bedrooms, three fireplaces, six bathrooms, and an enormous kitchen. When his father was alive, the place was vibrant and constantly filled with friends and relatives who treated it like a second home.

However, when his father passed on and Morris inherited his wealth, the party was clearly over. Both miserly and suspicious, Morris kicked everyone out and had all the rooms sealed off with the exception of the living room, one bedroom, one bathroom, and the kitchen. Under his ownership, what was once a pleasure palace became a virtual mausoleum.

He had no wife, children, or friends, which was just fine with him. He was perfectly content to be left alone in the dark with his anger and his booze. But that all changed the other night when he looked out his window and saw the hat and scarf on the Campbell snowman.

Although it had been thirty years, Morris never forgot Lucas' promise of revenge. He truly believed that Walks was a genuinely evil being and that he had been referring to the devil when he said that he had "powerful friends." With this in mind and with the sudden reappearance of the hat and scarf after so many years, he decided to keep a careful eye on the snowman just in case.

After placing a chair and end table next to the picture window, he spent every available moment watching the parade through his binoculars. At first, he told himself that he was acting paranoid and foolish, but when the Campbell snowman began mysteriously appearing at the front of the parade long after the crews had gone home and the ATV's were locked away in the DPW garage, he began to have second thoughts.

For one thing, he knew such movement wasn't possible. A snowman that size would require a team of three people and an ATV to move it from one place to another. So if Nick and his crew weren't involved, who was? Morris was determined to find out.

On the night of Ernie's death, he had just finished a late supper and had sat down to begin his usual routine. As he looked out over the lake, he saw that once again the Lead Snowman was nowhere to be found.

He immediately began scouring the area and soon came upon Ernie wandering out toward the middle of the lake. At first he thought that odd, especially since it was so late at night. But when he saw that the Lead Snowman was out there as well, he became curious and wondered what the old man was up to.

Then it hit him. "He's going to grab the hat and scarf!" he said with both surprise and admiration. He too, had considered going out there and taking the items but hadn't been able to muster up the courage. But now that Ernie was taking care of that problem for him, he decided that it called for a celebration. He immediately threw on his hat and coat and headed out to invite the old man back to the house for a drink.

Morris left through the door that faced the lake. He eased himself down the hill but stopped when he saw Ernie struggling with the scarf. "What in blazes is going on out there?" he muttered. Then he saw the old man slip and fall and heard the snapping of Ernie's neck. He gazed in horror as the old man's body jerked spastically then fell motionless.

Wide-eyed and in shock, Morris buried his face in his hands. At first, he was going to run back to the house and pretend he hadn't seen a thing. But lord! hadn't he been alone in the house long enough? No, he decided. He was going to do something. He was going out on the ice and help Ernie, maybe get him to a doctor, maybe it wasn't too late. Yes, sir! That's what he was going to do.

He slid his hands from his face and edged himself along the few remaining trees. Ernie was still a good distance away but as he drew nearer, he could clearly see the dark outline of the older man's body dangling inches above the ice.

The moon momentarily dipped behind the clouds. "Hold on, old fella," he said. "Help's on the way." Morris moved quickly along the part of his property that extended out on the lake and was about to step on the surface when the light of the moon returned.

The illumination swept across the ice, settling first on Ernie Campbell's remains.

There was no doubt the old man was dead. His face was purple and contorted into a gruesome death mask, his eyes bulged from their sockets like golf balls, and his tongue hung from his open mouth like a black leather strap. Even after seeing all this, Morris might have ventured a little closer, if for no other reason than to cut the body loose. But as moonlight continued its journey and settled upon the snowman, what Morris saw sent an electrical current up his spine. When he had first looked out from behind the branches, the snowman's face had been positioned toward Ernie. Now, he suddenly realized, the dark eyes of the snowman were staring directly at him!

Morris spun on his heels and dashed for his house. His heart was pounding so rapidly it felt like it was going to jump out of his chest.

Once inside, he slammed the door closed and locked it behind him. He threw off his coat and ran for the phone. He picked up the receiver, stared at the numbers, and decided to call...to call. Wait. Just whom was he going to call? The police? They'll never believe him. In fact, they might think he had something to do with Ernie's death. For an ambulance? No, Ernie was dead. He was sure of that.

He stared at the phone for a moment then quickly punched the number of someone he hadn't spoken to for quite a long time. The conversation was brief and clearly did not go the way he had anticipated. Furious, he slammed the receiver down. He shook his head, flopped down into his chair, and cautiously picked up the binoculars.

It was as he had feared. The snowman was still staring at him.

19

Roy had made arrangements with the funeral home early Tuesday morning and by seven p.m. that evening Ernie Campbell's body was lying in state for mourners to say their good-byes. Mike and Winks Shays were among the first to arrive. Mike went directly to the viewing room while Winks remained outside with Josh.

"I'm really sorry about your granddad," Winks said as they walked along the hallway.

Josh, dressed in his best (and only) suit, looked into the viewing room and watched the parade of mourners stop at the casket, pray for a moment, and then return to their seats. "Thanks, Winks," he said finally. "I appreciate you and your dad coming." His voice was strained. Winks could see that Josh was having a hard time dealing with this.

"I saw your grandfather at the lake during opening ceremonies, he looked fine then. Does anybody know what happened? Did he have another stroke?" Winks asked.

Josh shook his head. "I just can't talk about it right now, Winks, I'm sorry. I'm just...just...."

Winks saw the tears welling up in Josh's eyes and for a moment was startled that his hero was actually on the verge of crying. Josh crying? But Josh could handle anything. But then he realized that had someone he loved died so suddenly, he'd probably be crying too. Winks momentarily turned away to give Josh the privacy he needed to compose himself.

"Josh, I got to go in with my dad now," he said. "But we'll get together soon and we can talk this out, or just hang or do anything you want, okay, buddy?"

Josh sniffled twice and nodded. Winks smiled and went inside while Josh went to the men's room to put a little water on his face.

While Josh was washing up, a puffy-faced gentleman with long hair and stubble entered the viewing room and signed the guest book. It took several minutes before people realized that Morris Allison, the hermit of Little Pond Lake, was making a rare public appearance.

Taking his turn on line, Morris knelt at the side of the coffin and said a short prayer. When he was finished, he reached up, touched the arm of the deceased, then went over and sat down next to Mike Shays and Winks.

Mike was surprised that Morris had come. Personally, he didn't think that Morris cared about anyone, let alone Ernie.

"We have to talk," Morris said slowly and firmly.

Mike shook his head. "I know of no business between us, Allison."

"But...."

"Good day, sir," Mike said firmly making it clear he didn't want to hear anything Morris had to say. Shaking his head, Morris rose from his seat and left the viewing room.

Winks nudged his father. "Dad, what was that about?"

Mike glanced at the door and then the coffin. "Nothing, son," he replied.

As Josh was leaving the men's room, he saw Morris Allison walking toward him on his way to the exit. As they passed, Morris stopped for a moment and stared at Josh. "You don't know what you started, boy," he said and then swung open the exit door and left the building.

Started what? What was he talking about? Josh asked himself. Then he saw Winks barreling toward him.

"Oh man, Josh," he said, slightly out of breath.

"What?"

Winks rubbed his partially closed eye. "Something weird is going on. Primo weirdness."

"Winks, some other time," Josh said as he started toward the viewing room.

Winks ran up alongside him. "Josh! I'm not kidding. Old man Allison was just here."

Josh stopped. "I know. I just saw him and do you know what he said to me? He said, 'You don't know what you started, boy,' and then walked off. What do you make of that?"

Winks pulled Josh over to one of the benches in the hall. "My dad freaked out when he saw our snowman the other day. I mean he really lost it."

"My grandfather did too. We had to leave the parade early because of him. My father took us to a restaurant and when we got there my granddad starts drinking and talking all weird like. Then out of nowhere he shouts, 'That snowman is an abomination!' right in the middle of the restaurant. And then he starts going on about a man's responsibilities and that Walks was a rabid dog that had to be put down. I tell you, Winks, he was scaring the crap out of me. What's going on here?"

Winks shoved his hands in his pockets. "I'm not sure, but

things are starting to add up in a way I don't like. You probably don't see it yet because you're so upset."

"Spill it, Winks," Josh said coldly.

Winks had momentarily forgotten how Josh hated anyone beating around the bush. Josh was a man of action, a lion, and not one to be left hanging out on a limb. But Winks also remembered, that when in the presence of lions, one roars whether he is a lion or not.

"I won't tell you now," he replied, accentuating "won't" and proud that he didn't say "can't." "Not until I'm sure. But I'm beginning to think that maybe old man Allison was right. Maybe we did start something."

Now it was Josh's turn to mull things over. He was almost sure that Winks had concocted some bizarre theory that included ghosts, zombies, and other such nonsense but he was right about one thing. Ever since they took that old hat and scarf out of the attic and placed it on that snowman, events in the town were getting decidedly weirder, even for Sparks.

20

After he arrived home from Ernie's wake, Morris kicked the snow from his boots, placed his coat on the rack, and went over to the liquor cabinet to pour himself a drink.

"Damn fool!" he said aloud. "Wouldn't even talk to me."

Morris filled the glass with scotch and sat down in the chair that looked out over the parade. "Saw the whole thing from right here. Right from this very spot," he said to no one. "I'm trying to save peoples lives and this is how I get treated. Like some head case!"

He took a sip and brushed away the tiny droplets that had dribbled down his shirt. "Idiots, the whole damn town is filled with idiots!"

Morris crossed his legs and sank further down into his seat. He stopped his tirade just long enough to pick up the binoculars he kept on the end table and stare out at the parade. The ends of his mouth turned down as he focused on the Lead Snowman, which was once again positioned at the front of the parade. "That's you, Walks, yes, sir. That's you all right. And I'll tell you something else, Mr. Snowman, I know you can move. Ain't seen you actually do it yet. But I will. Yes, sir, I surely will."

With a snarl that looked as if it had been chiseled into his face, Morris continued to stare out at the Snowman's Parade.

Minutes drifted into hours yet Morris remained vigilant, eyes glued to the window. But as determined as he was, weariness and alcohol were beginning to take their toll. His eyes burned and his hands were cramping under the weight of the binoculars. Then something caught his attention. It was the Styrofoam Christmas balls that were strung around the speaker columns. They were swinging back and forth in the breeze.

Then it hit him. "Styrofoam!!" he thundered, jumping out of his chair. "Damn it all to hell!! That's how they did it. That's how they moved the snowman around! All you have to do is cover it with that plastic snow they use on storefront windows and there's no way you can tell a real one from a fake."

Morris spun around with his arms outstretched as if expecting to receive a thunderous round of applause for having solved the case of the movable snowman. There was, of course, no one there. Disappointed, he flopped back down in his chair.

That's it, though. Styrofoam can be made to any shape or size. Why, a child could pick it up and put it any place he wants in a matter of seconds.

Just when he thought he had it all figured out, he remembered Ernie. He saw Ernie die, no doubt about that. He pondered that thought for a moment.

Wait a minute. What if someone was standing beside the snowman, out of sight? Well, then, things might not be what they seem. A metal base with a pole could be used as an anchor for the Styrofoam balls. Just drill a hole through the bottom and middle shapes and place the head on top. But what about the head turning and facing him? Hold on, hold on, didn't I cover my face when Ernie died? Yes, sir, I believe I did! And if someone was there, beside the snow-

man, that same person could have moved the head in a matter of seconds.

It was possible. But he had to make sure.

He placed the binoculars on the table and hurriedly put on his coat and gloves. As he headed for the door, he stopped just long enough to pick up a poker from the fireplace. He had decided that if whoever killed Ernie was intending to ambush him as well, then that person was going to find himself with a dent in his head large enough to use as a spittoon.

Stepping out of the back door, Morris trudged through the snow and down the hill until he reached the lake. Once upon its surface, he moved cautiously, carefully listening to every sound. When he got to the parade, he looked through each row just to make sure he was alone. He checked the ice shack, and seeing that Nick had turned in for the night, proceeded to the front to inspect the Lead Snowman.

The few spots illuminating the area cast the figures in a gray light making them look more like statues or graveyard markers than snowmen. And even though Morris was convinced that the Campbell entry was nothing more than three Styrofoam balls stuck on top of each other, he was nonetheless intimidated by its size and its bizarre twisted grin.

"Well, big fella," he said shrugging off the initial shock. "Let's just see what you're really made of." Morris knelt down and ran his finger along the base, figuring it would be gluey and thick. It wasn't. Surprised, he jammed the poker through the center of the snowman and moved it around. There was no doubt now, it was real snow all right, and it didn't even have an icicle "backbone."

Morris sat back down on his heels, confused. He shook his head and as he glanced down on the ice, he could have swore he saw the snowman's shadow move. Curious, he looked up and the sight that greeted him made his heart begin to pound and his hands shake so that he nearly dropped the poker.

Somehow, the snowman's gold baton had disappeared and in its place was a frozen tree branch.

In a panic, Morris jumped up, closed his eyes, and swung at the head with the poker.

Somehow, he missed, or at least it appeared that he did. The momentum spun him around, causing him to lose his balance and fall to the ground. He rolled over several times to give himself distance. He immediately got up, and once again, the snowman was standing right in front of him.

"You…can…move," Morris whispered. "You can move! I was right all along!" Morris stepped back.

But how? A man in a costume? No. Not possible. I jammed the poker right through the middle. No man could fit in there. Case closed.

As he stared into the snowman's face, he could almost feel Walks' presence staring back at him. "Even if I have to crawl back from the deepest pit in Hell," he had said. "I will have my revenge on you!" Morris looked down and noticed his hand was shaking. Embarrassed, he took a deep breath and steadied himself. Then he looked up at the snowman and addressed his hated enemy.

"Well, well, Lucas," he said coldly. "It appears you kept your promise after all, yes, sir! Said you'd come back to get us and well, here you are. Well, I ain't afraid of you. I wasn't then and I ain't now, no, sir!"

True to his word, Morris tightened his grip on the poker and raised it above his head. Just as he was about to bring it down, large cracks suddenly appeared in the ice beneath his feet. Realizing the danger, Morris dropped down and spread himself out on the frozen surface.

"No, no, no, Mr. Snowman," he said. "I know all about the lake and its tricks and I know how to get around them." Morris then began pushing himself backward, inching his way toward the street.

"You might think you've won but you ain't. I'll be back at daylight to finish you off. Yes sir! You can bet on that."

Morris continued inching toward shore. He could hear the ice cracking all around but he remained confident. He was nearing the street and would soon be home free.

Suddenly a large chunk of ice collapsed into the icy waters directly beneath his head. His heart raced but he kept his eyes on the snowman. Reaching out like a blind man, he carefully felt around the area of the hole and breathed a sigh of relief when he realized that it wasn't big enough for him to fall through. Nervous laughter welled up in his throat.

"Not good enough, Lucas ol' boy," he said, almost chuckling. "Not nearly good enough." Morris was about to resume edging himself backward when he heard the waters inside the hole begin to churn.

As he glanced down, something shot out of the hole and wrapped itself around his head. In blind panic, Morris jerked from side to side, trying to break free. Whatever it was that had him, it was white and dotted with gray spots. At first, he thought they were birch tree branches. But that didn't make any sense. He looked again.

Arms!!? Skeletal Arms!!??

Morris propped his right hand under his shoulder and tried to pull free. His legs kicked wildly but the slippery ice made it impossible to get leverage. His chin was pressed against the ice hole. The water slapped his face once, then again.

Something grabbed his left ear and spun him to the side

knocking his right arm out from under him. The poker went flying from his hand and fell into the water. He opened his mouth to scream but his head was immediately yanked below the surface. He gazed into the water and was met by the black eye sockets of human skulls. The ice began to reform and tighten around his throat. His hands couldn't feel the edge of the hole anymore. The skulls continued to stare as the darkness began to overtake him.

This can't be happening!!

This can't be happening!

But it was.

21

The next morning Ritchie Parker, Sheriff Parker's son, came to work early so he could get the maintenance on the snowmen finished before Nick woke up. He figured that if he could do that, his boss would have no choice but to stop thinking of him as a slacker and a goof-off.

He would start with the Lead Snowman and the others in front. He knew those were the ones Nick was most concerned about.

After he parked his truck, he opened the DPW garage door, picked up his bag, and set out on his ATV. As he approached the parade, he saw what looked to be a pair of legs sticking out from just beyond the front of the Campbell snowman. At first, he thought it was a trick, one of his co-workers pulling a prank. But as he drew nearer, the smile he was wearing was replaced by a look of genuine concern.

When he got to the front, he climbed off his ATV and went over to investigate. Once he got close enough to the figure to see the head....

Ritchie, forgetting about the ATV, sprinted off the lake and ran across Shore Road to the pay phone. It rang several times before a groggy Sheriff Parker picked it up.

"Hello?" he said in a half-asleep voice.

"Dad, it's Ritchie! I'm down at the lake, Snowman's Parade! Dude's got his head stuck! Bad, really, really bad! Flat-out on the lake!"

The sheriff, unable to understand a single word his son had said, pulled the phone from his ear. "Ritchie!" he said talking down to the receiver. "For heaven's sake, take it easy. Now son, in simple English, what's the matter?"

"Okay, okay."

The sheriff heard his son take a deep breath. "Dad," he said calmly, "there's a dead guy on the lake. His head is frozen in the ice."

The first thing Sheriff Parker did after hearing the news was to tell Ritchie to wake Pederuco and instruct him to place one of the large canvass tents they used to cover the concession stands at night over the body and to await the arrival of the deputies and the EMS squad. Then he immediately called his office and instructed them to get out to the parade. "Close everything off," he said. "No one goes in or out, no one talks to the press."

When the sheriff arrived, there were a number of official vehicles lined up across Shore Road. He was greeted by several deputies who let him through the blockade, apprised him of the situation, and led him to the crime scene. He was relieved to see that Pederuco had the tent set up over the body so at least he wouldn't have to deal with gawkers and newspaper photographers.

As he walked across the ice, he saw his boy standing over on the side surrounded by his co-workers, all of whom looked as shaken as Ritchie. He decided it would be best not to approach his son now and instead waved and flashed him the "in a minute" sign. Besides, he wanted to see the body first. From what his deputies had told him, this was going to be a long day.

He pulled back the flap of the tent, walked in and gazed down at the remains, covered by a blue plastic sheet. "Okay," he said, "what do we have here?"

One of the EMS people pulled back the plastic. "White male, probably in his mid-fifties. Looks like he's been dead several hours."

The sheriff looked down at the corpse. Shaking his head, he turned to the deputy and EMS attendants. "Somebody explain this to me," he said. "How could this have happened?"

The deputy shrugged. "Sheriff, we have no idea."

"I'll tell you one thing," a voice said from behind him. "What we are looking at is simply not possible." The voice was that of Nick Pederuco, who had walked into the tent moments after Parker.

The sheriff looked at Nick and then to the others. "Do we at least know who he is?"

The deputy shook his head. "No. We checked his pockets. No ID. No nothing."

"Very well, then," he said taking off his hat and pushing back his hair. "Dig him out of there. But first get pictures. I'm sure there are going to be a lot of questions asked about this."

The sheriff stepped outside and went over to talk to Ritchie and his co-workers. Unfortunately, they added little to what he already knew. But there was something Nick had said earlier. Something that had stuck in his head.

He saw Nick walking back toward the ice shack and called him over. Together they strolled around the perimeter of the crime scene, away from the deputies and the EMS.

"You said what happened in there wasn't possible. What's so impossible about it?"

Nick studied the sheriff to see if he was serious. "Are you kidding?" Nick asked. "There's a man in there with his head imbedded in solid ice and you ask what's so impossible about it?"

"Well, indulge me."

Nick took a deep breath. "Well, for starters, it wasn't that cold last night. It fact, it was barely freezing. So even if he dug a hole, and then stuck his head into it until he drowned, the water shouldn't be frozen. And two," he continued, "did you notice the texture of the ice surrounding the man's head?"

The sheriff admitted that he had not.

"Well I did," Nick said. "And the texture is the exact same as the surrounding ice for at least ten feet. I measured it myself before I set up the tent."

"Which means?"

Nick put his fingers to his forehead as he tried to formulate the words necessary to explain how bizarre this situation was. "Okay," he said, "this is how it works. When water freezes, it forms tiny lines and air bubbles that create a pattern, like fingerprints. When the ice within that area is broken and refreezes it forms a completely different pattern because it froze at a different time and the conditions were not the same. What I'm saying, sheriff, is that there is no break anywhere in the pattern. None. Which means someone would have had to dig a hole ten feet wide and two feet deep and then lower him from something like a crane head first into the water, wait until the area around it refroze, THEN lower the rest of the body on top of the refrozen surface. What do you think the odds are that that actually happened?"

The sheriff was not amused.

Nick stuck his hands in his pockets. "Look, I know I come over a bit rough at times, but Alvin, I've been working DPW for a lot of years. And this might sound like bragging but nobody knows this lake better than I do. And I'm telling you, whatever happened to that guy in there is beyond any natural lake occurrence. And we both know there's considerable latitude given to what's considered 'natural' around here, especially when it comes to the lake."

The sheriff didn't argue the point. He knew that Nick was referring to the lake's violent history and the fact that an unusually large number of people had mysteriously disappeared out on its surface over the years. But before he could question Pederuco any further, he heard someone calling him.

"Sheriff, can I see you for a moment?" the deputy asked, waving from the tent.

The sheriff and Nick walked over to join the others inside. The body had been freed and Alvin didn't need anyone to tell him who it was. "Morris Allison," he said quietly. "Geez."

He pulled the plastic sheet back over the body. "Well," he said, "we're not going to know what really happened here until we get an autopsy report. Anyone have any ideas or comments?"

One of the EMS men shrugged. "The guy reeks of booze. He was definitely plastered when he died."

The sheriff looked down at the plastic sheet covering Allison's remains. "So, you're suggesting that he wandered out here drunk, fell, and froze to death?"

"He wouldn't be the first rummy to wind up that way," the EMS man replied.

Nick heard what had been said and looked at them both as if they were out of their minds. "What are you talking about? Drunk or not, his head was frozen in solid ice. How do you explain that?"

"I don't know, Nick!" the sheriff replied sharply. "What I do know is that Allison's been living alone in that old house over there for nearly thirty years. He drank himself stupid day in and day out, had no friends, no family, and no job. Who knows what a man like that is capable of? Hell, maybe he was ice fishing and fell in."

Nick gave him a "What are you, crazy?" look, but Parker ignored it. Instead, he had a question of his own for the head of the DPW. "You were here last night, didn't you see or hear anything?"

Pederuco shoved his hands in his pockets and shook his head.

The sheriff turned and addressed everyone in the tent. "Okay, until we hear from the coroner, I want this to be labeled as death due to accidental drowning."

"But sheriff," both Nick and one of the deputies said almost in unison.

"Listen to me. We are at the beginning of tourist season and the last thing we need is a lot of unsubstantiated rumor. Now you all know that the Snowman's Parade is damn near the sole support of this area and brings in a considerable amount of money. Do any of you want to see that money dry up because of some clumsy drunk?"

Nick and the others admitted that they did not.

"So, are we agreed that until we know otherwise, this is to be treated like any other drowning case?"

No one said anything.

The sheriff adjusted his hat. "I'll take that as a yes. In the meantime, Nick, I think it would be a good idea to double-check the thickness of the ice in this area. Just until we get a handle on this thing."

22

They say you can't keep a secret in a small town and that certainly seemed to be the case at the Sparks Central School the following day. Although Sheriff Parker had done everything possible to keep the circumstances surrounding Morris Allison's death quiet, rumors spread like wildfire. Billy Curtis had heard from a friend of a friend that one of the deputies had been ambushed and killed. Another rumor had a small boy falling through the ice and drowning while another claimed that someone had died trying to destroy the Lead Snowman.

Winks didn't know if any of the rumors were true, but there was no doubt in his mind that something had happened out on the lake yesterday. The hushed whispers of the teaching staff and the fact that Shore Road had been closed off for the better part of the day was almost confirmation in itself.

After Winks had returned home from school, he took off his coat and tossed his book bag on the staircase. As he walked past the living room, he saw that the phone-answering machine light was blinking. Hoping that Josh had called, he rushed in and pushed the button. It wasn't Josh's voice that played back, however, but that of his father's long-time friend, Theo McKay.

Mike, this is Theo. I left a message at your office but in case you didn't get it, I need to speak with you right away. Listen, Morris Allison phoned me the other night, very agitated. Said he saw Ernie Campbell strangled by Walks' old scarf. He sounded a bit drunk so I told him to go sleep it off, then hung up. Well, this afternoon, Ritchie Parker drops off his truck at my shop for some repair work. We get to talking and he tells me that Ernie WAS strangled by Walks' scarf and what's more, yesterday morning Morris was found dead in front of the Lead Snowman with his entire head frozen in the ice. Now, I think we both know what this means. Call me.

"Josh's grandfather was strangled by the snowman's scarf? And now Morris Allison is dead, too? Oh, this isn't good," he said as he sat down on the couch.

As he replayed the phone message in his head it suddenly struck him as odd that Morris Allison would call Theo McKay in the first place. In all the years that Theo and his father had been friends, Winks couldn't remember Theo McKay ever mentioning Morris Allison's name. In fact, as far as he knew, the two of them didn't really even know each other. Then he remembered Morris approaching his father at Ernie Campbell's wake. That didn't seem to make any sense either. Could it be that Morris had seen who strangled Josh's grandfather? And if he had, why didn't he just call the police or Josh's dad?

Winks shook his head and decided to put it out of his mind until he had a chance to speak with Josh. Maybe together they could figure out what was going on.

As the hours ticked by Winks became bored and restless and began looking for something to do. He wandered around the house and was about to turn on the television when his eyes settled on the attic door.

Hmmmm. Haven't been up there in a while.

He momentarily considered having a look but then remembered that the attic, for the most part, contained nothing of interest.

But his curiosity was beginning to get the better of him. Maybe, like Josh's house, there was a secret room or, even better, maybe his dad had done the Christmas shopping and hidden presents up there. Well, the possibility of finding Christmas presents wasn't very likely, he decided. Not when your father can stash anything he wants in his office at work.

Winks reached for the knob and turned it.

It was dark inside and he could smell the mustiness and age even at the bottom step. Still, it was an adventure, so he clicked on the single overhead light and began climbing the stairs.

After pushing aside several cobwebs, and giving his eyes and nose a chance to adjust to the dim lighting and stale air, he began his search. He spent ten minutes checking every possible nook and cranny and even tapped on wall panels for hollow sounds, but found nothing. Eventually he gave up, realizing his quest for secret passageways and hidden holiday gifts was just a waste of time.

Disappointed, he grabbed an old box, plopped down on the floor, and opened it. Inside were hundreds of pictures. Old pictures. Pictures that had a brownish tint to them.

After sifting through countless photos of friends, buildings, and farm animals, he came upon one that immediately grabbed his attention. In that particular photograph, somebody had drawn a black X on the face of what appeared to be one of the farmhands. He thought that strange and tried to make out the person's face, but the deep X in the photo made it impossible.

Winks then dug down to the bottom of the box hoping to find

something equally as intriguing. As he rummaged around, his hand brushed against what felt like a metal frame. He pushed the other photos aside and pulled it out.

It was a frame, and a gold one at that. Using his shirttail to wipe off the dust and dirt from the glass, he discovered that it was an eight-by-ten black and white photo of a woman. She appeared to be in her twenties and had an unmistakably sweet and loving face. Winks was captivated by the picture and was dying to know who she was. He quickly dug through the rest of the photos hoping to find another, but it soon became apparent that that was the only one.

Winks picked up the stacks of pictures he had scattered on the floor and dropped them back in the box, disappointed because without additional information he would probably never know who the smiling lady was.

He carefully placed the framed photo in his lap and stared at it. Then, without thinking, he turned it over and removed the cardboard holder.

There was writing on the back of the photo. It was faded but he still could make it out.

To Michael, my future husband. All my love, now and forever, Martha.

Winks flipped the photo back and forth, alternating between the picture and the inscription.

An enraged suitor, the book had said.

I think we both know what this means. Call me.

"Oh dad!" he said, dropping the picture back into his lap.

It all fit now.

Winks reached in the box one more time and pulled out the photo with the X on it.

He now knew whose face the X was drawn through. Although

he hadn't noticed them before, the black floppy hat and scarf were a dead give away.

Mike had gotten Theo's message from his secretary and had agreed to meet him after work at the Adirondack Diner. After they settled in at a booth in the back, Theo took a sip of his coffee then got right down to business.

"I've been giving this a lot of thought," he said staring into Mike's pale blue eyes. "And I'm beginning to believe that Morris was right. Somehow, Walks *has* come back."

Theo instantly put up his hand to ward off Mike's certain interruption. "Just hear me out," he continued. "Look, the way both Ernie and Morris died is simply too bizarre to write off as accidents. I mean, just think about it. Ernie's body was found dangling from the snowman's scarf just inches above the surface. Second, Morris's head is embedded in solid ice. There is absolutely no way the ice could have frozen around Morris's head in just a few hours. No way! What's more, I see a pattern emerging, one that points directly to Lucas."

Mike tilted his head. "Pattern?" he replied. "What pattern?"

Theo looked around to make sure no one was listening in. "Think back to that night. It was Ernie who placed the noose around Walks' neck. And it was Ernie who cut him down. How does Ernie die? He was hanged. Now Morris, well, he got a little freaked out after Lucas croaked, remember? He wouldn't even touch the body. Soon afterward, he turned to drink and locked himself away in that big house. How did Morris die? With his head buried in the proverbial sand."

"That sounds like a bit of a stretch to me, Theo." Mike said.

Theo moved in closer. "It's not when you really think about it.

We both know what kind of man Lucas was and you can bet that if he has come back for revenge, he'd make a point of letting us know it.

"Which brings me to another point. I was talking to Lech Skorski at the supermarket the other day and he told me that his snowman originally won the Lead Snowman position but that someone had destroyed it and replaced it with the Campbells.

"Look, Mike, all I'm asking is that you put the pieces together. For thirty years, nothing happens. Then just days after Walks' hat and scarf reappear, two of us are dead. Both killed in the most bizarre ways imaginable and in the vicinity of the Lead Snowman. Seriously, what if, in the next few days, something happened to me? Would you still refuse to believe that Walks is responsible?"

Mike finished up his coffee. "You seem to forget, Theo, that Walks is no longer among the living."

"And you, Mike," Theo immediately replied, "seem to forget that our little lake has the most horrifying and violent history imaginable. People talk about haunted houses and haunted graveyards all the time and no one blinks an eye. Let's face it, if any place could be haunted, that damn lake certainly qualifies. I mean what about the old bones?"

Mike smirked and shook his head. "C'mon, everybody knows that those 'old bones' are nothing more than birch tree branches that snapped off and fell into the lake. All that talk about them being the skeletal remains of the renegades is just nonsense."

Theo sighed when he saw he wasn't getting through. "Mike, let me ask you a question. How did you feel when you saw Walks' hat and scarf on the snowman? Did you want to rip them off and destroy them? I know I did. Well, I believe that's what Ernie and Morris had intended to do. The problem was, they weren't careful and forgot who they were dealing with."

Mike looked out the window. "I'm sorry, Theo. I'll admit it's pretty unsettling, even spooky, but it's got to be a coincidence. But, I'll tell you this. If you want to go down there and grab that hat and scarf, I'll gladly go with you. In fact," Mike said rising from his seat, "let's go take care of it right now."

Theo shook his head. "Can't. Thought about it myself but with two deaths in two days, you can bet the police are going to keep a close eye on the parade, at least for the time being. I'm glad that you agree that the hat and scarf have got to go, but we can't do it tonight."

"Ok then, when?"

"Soon."

After Theo left, Mike sat there thinking about what he had done thirty years ago. How he had stood over the closed casket of the one woman he would ever truly love. A casket closed because the wounds inflicted were so savage that no amount of makeup or cosmetics could mask the brutality of the assault. And, finally, the sacred promise he made to her to see that the person responsible paid for his crime. He had kept that promise.

Walks, he remembered, made a promise, too. And, like Mike, it was beginning to look as if he was just as determined to keep it.

23

It was finally Friday and Winks was anxious for the school day to end so he could get together with Josh and tell him all that had happened.

The lunch bell rang and as Winks walked down the stairs toward the cafeteria, a hand suddenly appeared on his shoulder. His heart jumped and he quickly turned to see who it was.

"Josh!" he said excitedly. "I thought I wasn't going to see you until this afternoon."

Josh shrugged. "I didn't want to spend another day moping around the house, so after the funeral, I talked my dad into letting me go to school."

"Oh man, I am sooooo glad to see you!" Winks said as he fought the urge to wrap his arms around his friend and give him a big hug.

Josh smiled at Winks' enthusiasm. "Good to see you, too, pal. What's new?"

Winks shook his head. "An awful lot, Josh," he replied. "We've got to talk."

While sitting in Winks' bedroom after school, the boys began to compare notes. Winks was astonished to hear that not only had Josh's grandfather been strangled by Walks' scarf, but that he had been found out in the middle of the lake hanging from it in front of the Lead Snowman. Josh was equally as astonished when Winks told him about Morris Allison.

Convinced that they were on to something, Josh quickly told Winks the whole story about his conversation with his grandfather at the restaurant and when he was finished, Winks informed Josh about the inscription on the back of Martha Cleary's picture, the X'd out photo, and the phone message from Theo McKay.

The boys sat quietly for several minutes as they mulled over this new information. Both were convinced that they had all of the pieces of the puzzle; the only problem now was to put them together. Surprisingly, it was Winks who figured it out first and he knew Josh was going to bristle when he told him what he had come up with.

"Josh," he said solemnly. "I think I know who hanged Lucas Walks."

"Who?"

Winks nervously rolled his hands together, then took a deep breath. "Lucas Walks was hanged by my dad, Morris Allison, Theo McKay, and...and your grandfather."

Josh's eyes went hard. "That's not true!"

Winks squirmed in his seat. "It all adds up, Josh. Your father's story about the trial, the library book, what your grandfather said, the pictures, and the phone call from Theo McKay. Just think about it." Winks then looked into Josh's eyes. "You know I'm right."

Josh's anger slowly drained from his face. He bit down on his lip and after a moment, nodded. He had wracked his brain trying to avoid that same conclusion, but there was no sense in denying it any longer.

"I think I knew my grandfather was involved when we talked about Walks at the restaurant," he said. "He didn't come right out and say he hanged the guy but the way he spoke, I tell you, I could almost see it in his eyes. But at the time I just didn't want to believe it. He was my grandfather, so…."

"I know what you mean," Winks replied. "I felt the same way after I found the pictures."

"Fire Phasers," said Jean-Paul as he edged across his perch.

Winks looked over at the cage then got up and filled the bird's water bowl.

"What I don't understand," Josh said, "is why they didn't simply grab Walks and drag him back to town? I mean, I know he got away with killing Martha Cleary but he was still wanted in Michigan."

Winks closed the cage door and sat back down. "Maybe they were afraid he'd get off like he did here and in Georgia and then come back to get them for turning him in."

Josh shook his head. "I don't think he would have come back."

Winks threw up his arms. "What do you mean, Josh, buddy? He HAS come back. Your grandfather and Mr. Allison are proof of that. One by one, Walks is killing the guys who hanged him!"

Josh rubbed his forehead. Could Winks be right? Could the ghost of a serial killer be residing in their snowman?

"Mikey, Mikey, Mikeeeyyy!" Jean-Paul squawked enthusiastically.

Both boys turned toward the bird. "Wow, I never heard him say that before," Winks said.

Josh suddenly remembered that's what his father said Lucas Walks called Mike Shays. He didn't think it was important, so he hadn't mentioned that part of the story to Winks. Now he wondered if he should. After mulling it over, he decided not to, things were crazy enough and he was sure that his young friend would read too much into it.

Winks switched over to the chair at his computer desk. "Remember how your grandfather kept going on about how the hat and scarf had to be burned?"

"Yeah."

"Well, I think I figured out why. You said that right after he saw our snowman, he got all nervous and started drinking. Maybe he was afraid this was going to happen."

That made sense to Josh. "You might be onto something," he said. "My grandfather truly believed that the lake was haunted and it really shook him when he saw Walks' hat and scarf on the Lead Snowman. Maybe he snuck down there that night to burn them. And maybe that's what Morris Allison was trying to do, too," he added.

It all seemed to be coming together but, as it did, one frightening thought occurred to Winks. "Josh, now that your grandfather and Morris Allison are dead, he's going to go after Theo McKay and my dad! Oh man, I've got to stop him!"

"*We've* got to stop him. The question is when?"

"Tonight?" Winks asked, surprised at his own bravery.

"No," Josh said shaking his head. "Everything might look like it's back to normal but you can bet the cops and Pederuco will still be on the lookout. Let's take a ride down there tomorrow morning. Then we can decide what to do."

That evening Nick sat in the ice shack staring at the small portable television. His eyes were glazed and the fact that there was only static snow on the screen was not registering in his head. He was sweating profusely, although the heat was off and the ice shack cold. His hands were wrapped around the arms of the chair so tightly, his knuckles were white and his forearms shook. His eyes were open, yet did not blink and did not see.

Then suddenly, he bolted upright, looked around, and drew several gasping breaths. He turned from side to side, his ears straining for the slightest sound. Leaping out of the chair, he ran to the window. He scoured the outside but saw nothing but row after row of dimly lit snowmen staring blindly out toward the street. All was quiet, dead quiet. There wasn't a sound anywhere other than the steady ticking of the quartz clock on the wall and the static hiss of the television.

As the cobwebs fell away, he began to feel the cold. He turned on the heater, bundled himself in a blanket, and sat down on the bed. It was several minutes before he was warm enough to stop shivering and several more before he could finally accept the fact that the voices in his head, the voices he had been hearing on and off over the last few days, had finally gone silent.

It was the night before Opening Day Ceremonies when they first appeared. In the beginning, it sounded like there was a radio or television on somewhere nearby. Nick didn't pay much attention, suspecting that Ritchie had somehow screwed up the signal to the speaker columns and picked up some late night talk show.

When Ritchie showed up for work the next day, Nick had him tear down the music system and double check everything. Ritchie did but could find nothing wrong. When the voices returned the second night, the night Ernie Campbell died, Nick phoned the Municipal Center in the morning and instructed them to send over one of the people from the company that built their microwave towers and radio antennas.

That afternoon Nick met with their chief engineer. The man

spent hours checking every component, but like Ritchie, found nothing wrong.

He explained to Nick that the holiday music came from a 90 minute tape with a pre-programmed timer that turned the music on and off at scheduled intervals. It didn't involve radio and the speakers were designed to lock out everything but the direct signal from the tape.

Still, each night the voices called to him. Growing closer and louder. And now, in addition, he was beginning to suffer from black-outs. Whole sections of time where he didn't know where he had been or what he had done. Tonight had been one of those nights.

Nick closed his eyes and rubbed his temples. The shack was finally warming up so he shrugged off the blankets and thought about Ernie and Morris.

He could accept the fact that they were dead. People dying or disappearing was not unusual at Little Pond. But that their deaths were so bizarre as to be almost supernatural frightened him. It was as if the rules that Nick and his watery adversary had adhered to for so long were breaking down, and that whatever demonic force held the lake in its grasp was, perhaps like himself, going mad.

24

Several hours later, after he was sure that Nick had turned in for the night, Theo McKay drove down the dark roads that led to the lake. Mike had called him earlier in the day and said that he thought Sunday evening would be the best time to go ahead with their plan to grab the hat and scarf. Theo pretended to agree and didn't let on that he had already made up his mind to take care of it himself, tonight.

Theo didn't like deceiving his best friend but felt Mike was a little *too* skeptical about the possibility of Lucas coming back and that skepticism might make him a liability instead of an asset should anything...well, unusual happen.

Besides, it would take two minutes, tops. In and out, get the job done. Then tomorrow he would tell Mike. Mike would be mad for having been left out, then he would get over it and life would return to normal.

When Theo arrived at the lake, the place was deserted. Only the small overhead lamps atop the speaker columns and the street-lights of Shore Road lit the area.

He pulled his car up behind the pizza stand and looked out on the surface, carefully checking the ice shack for any sign of life.

Seeing it dark, he shut off the headlights and climbed out of the car. He kept the engine running, though, just in case.

As he stepped out on the ice, he took one last quick look around then headed out toward the parade. He strode confidently, refusing to let any thought of failure or last minute jitters overcome his resolve. In the distance, he could see the Lead Snowman standing in its usual spot, almost as if waiting for him.

There was no doubt in Theo's mind that he would succeed where Morris and Ernie had failed. He was sure they had made the mistake of wanting to savor the moment, to relish their one last victory over Walks. This over-confident attitude, he believed, had probably cost them their lives.

Although it had been thirty years, Theo never forgot the beating he received and how close he came to being that SOB's final victim. He shuddered when he thought what might have happened if Mike hadn't snuck up on Walks from behind....

Theo wasn't going to savor anything.

In and out. In and out. Get the job done.

The wind began to blow and Theo raised his collar to ward it off. Already he was growing impatient. The Lead Snowman was only about twenty-five to thirty feet from the street, yet he felt as if he had been walking for a half an hour. He checked his watch. Almost two-thirty. No, he was right on schedule. Probably just nerves.

The wind was rapidly increasing in strength, blowing snow in every direction. He suddenly became confused, not quite sure of where he was. He stopped for a moment to get his bearings and to wait for the wind and snow to subside. When it finally did, Theo found himself standing right in front of the snowman.

Although mildly surprised, Theo was almost tempted to grin and make some remark, some biting comment or barb just to let

Walks know he was about to be on the losing side once again, but quickly changed his mind.

In and out. In and out. Get the job done.

Summoning his courage, he reached up and grasped the brim of the black floppy hat. His jaw fell when the brim disintegrated into a handful of black snow. He pulled back, startled, yet reached out a second time. Again the brim edge disintegrated and the dark snow fell to the ground. It was like trying to pick up a sandcastle with a fork. The more he tried, the more it fell apart. Annoyed, he reached for the scarf. It, too, turned to grainy snow in his grasp.

"What is this!?" he shouted.

Frustrated and determined, he reached up with both hands and tried again. And again they crumbled, only this time, when the snow slipped from his fingers, it didn't fall to the ice. Instead, it swirled around him and then rose and reattached itself to the area from where it had been removed.

Theo then looked into the face of the snowman and his breath caught in his throat. The black eyes were melting, the carrot was now a green and brown stub, and jagged icicles were forming around the mouth.

"No!!!" Theo screamed and in blind panic attacked the snowman with his fists. Each place struck exploded in a fine mist and swirled around him. He flailed wildly until snow was flying all over and he could no longer see what he was hitting.

The wind began to howl, and then scream. The temperature was dropping rapidly and Theo's lips began to freeze and his lungs burn. In desperation, he took a few steps back then charged into the snowman like a linebacker hoping to knock it over. Instead of toppling, it exploded. Theo was thrown into the air and fell backward into the snow.

Dazed, he shook his head and looked around trying to figure out what had happened and where he had landed. He couldn't even see the snowmen. The snow was falling so hard that everything was white in all directions.

He staggered to his feet and began waving his arms in front of his face, hoping somehow to push back the falling snow like a curtain. Strangely enough, it seemed to work. In the distance, he saw a dark figure moving across the surface.

"Help me. Help me!" Theo shouted as he climbed to his feet.

The snow was already up to his calves but he dragged himself closer toward the dark silhouette.

"Which way to the street?!" he shouted. "Hello? I can't see which way I'm going. Can you point me to the street?"

There was no answer. Theo continued slogging toward the figure, thinking that perhaps he hadn't heard him because of the wind. The falling snow obstructed his vision for a few seconds but, when it cleared enough for him to see, a scream welled up in his throat. The figure he had been running toward was the Lead Snowman.

And it appeared to be smiling.

Panic overcame him. "In and out. In and out!" he shouted, although the phrase no longer had any meaning. Seeing what he thought was a light somewhere in the distance, Theo took off, his legs pumping up and down through the snow, his chest heaving.

The wind screeched by him like a freight train and howled in his ears. Every instinct told him to keep running. He tried. But the snow...! There was so much snow! And suddenly, the light he had been running toward disappeared.

The snowfall tapered off, revealing a large drift directly in front of him. He tried to stop, but a powerful gust of wind shoved him from behind and knocked him into it.

Theo lifted his head, spun around, and shook the snow from his face. While trying to catch his breath, he sat up and saw what looked like large ice crystals forming around his feet. He tried to pull loose but the crystals had already solidified, freezing his boots to the surface. He made a fist and attempted to break up the ice but the snow continued to accumulate, making each blow less effective. With the snow rapidly covering his bootlaces, it was impossible for him to untie them. "Help!" he shouted, but the wind drowned out his cries. He stood up and frantically tried to pull his boots free but the ice was locked tight around them.

The snow was becoming thicker, slapping against him like blobs of plaster. He bent over and tried to push the snow from his legs, but it simply blew back and reattached itself. As he straightened up, he felt the weight of the snow accumulating on his shoulders and head. He moved to brush his shoulders when he saw that the snow was beginning to change color and form. His eyes widened as it mutated into a brown and red scarf. Immediately, he began clawing at it but the snow simply reformed as quickly as he brushed it off. As he searched for something to help him break free, what appeared to be a black brim began forming on his head.

With increasing panic, he twisted and tried to shake the snow loose but it clung to him like cement. It was like a living thing that was now crawling up his legs. He let out a scream but it was immediately muffled as ice crystals rapidly filled his mouth.

The snow on the lake in front of him began to blow away revealing his mirror image on the icy surface. Looking down he could see that icicles were forming around the edges of his mouth. He attempted to reach up and remove them but discovered that his right arm was covered in snow and he was barely able to move it. Slowly a baton took shape in his hand.

He couldn't even hear his own cries for help because his ears were now covered by thick clumps of slush.

Muffled screams echoed in his head as the snow continued to wrap itself around him, changing color, and taking the shape of a neon blue band jacket. With his remaining free arm, he frantically tried to rip the snow from his body. His left eye then closed and as he looked down, he saw what looked like a lump of coal forming over it.

He began to shiver uncontrollably. His body jerked and shook but the snow only wrapped tighter around him. His remaining arm grew heavy and dropped to his side. The weight of the snow continued to press down on him, making it impossible for him to move. With his one remaining eye, he could see the scarf flapping around his face and the gold baton reflecting the dim overhead lights. He tried to scream again but his mouth was now totally covered in snow and ice.

With what felt like the tiny legs of a million spiders, the grainy snow crept up alongside his face and edged toward his nose.

Realizing that if his nose were covered he would immediately suffocate, he began breathing furiously through his nostrils, hoping that his hot breath would melt the snow before it could obstruct his passageways.

In and out. In and out.

It seemed to be working. Focusing all his attention on that one simple act, Theo continued breathing rapidly. He glanced down at the reflection just long enough to see the snow begin to form around the corner of his eye and a brown and green stub extend from the bridge of his nose.

In and out. In and out!

He attempted to breathe even faster as the snow blotted out his vision. Suddenly one of his nostrils clogged.

In and out!!!
Then the other.
In...
and...
Out!!...
In......
and...

25

Early Saturday morning Nick Pederuco was sitting on the cot in the ice shack staring at the window. He held his coffee cup tightly in his hand and read what was written on the frosty pane over and over. The word was *Sacrifices.* And it was written in his own hand.

He hadn't remembered writing it. In fact, he couldn't remember waking up at all last night.

There was a knock on the door. Nick jerked and nearly spilled his coffee.

"It's Ritchie," came the voice.

As far as he knew, Ritchie wasn't scheduled to work until Monday. He dashed over to the window and quickly erased the words with his hand. He then took a deep breath, opened the door, and let the kid in.

Ritchie smiled, looked around, and then suddenly became confused.

"Isn't Mr. McKay here?"

Nick put his coffee down next to the hotplate. "No, why would McKay be here?"

Ritchie shrugged. "Well, I was coming by to see if one of the crew had called in sick, or if you needed an extra hand this weekend, and I saw his car outside parked behind the pizza stand. He did some work on my truck yesterday and I owe him a couple of dollars on the bill. So I figured I'd kill two birds with one stone and settle up with him now."

Nick shook his head. "I haven't seen him. Maybe he had car trouble and called a cab."

"I don't think so," Ritchie replied. "The engine is still running."

Nick's heart sank and the coffee in his stomach was threatening to come up. "His car's running? Why would he leave his car running?"

"Beats me," Ritchie replied.

Nick put on his coat and headed for the door. "Let's check this out."

It was as Ritchie had said. Theo McKay's car was parked behind the pizza stand with the engine still going. The door was unlocked so Nick opened it and looked in. The inside was warm, almost hot, and the dashboard gaslight was flashing. The tank was near empty.

Nick shut off the engine and took the keys. "Ain't this the damnedest thing?" he said closing the door. "Why would Theo leave his car running, especially when it's almost out of gas?"

Ritchie wrapped his hands around his waist. "It's probably nothing, Nick," he said trying to make smoke rings with his frosty breath. "Mr. McKay probably met someone, went with them, and forgot about the car."

Nick smirked. "If that were the case, why hide it behind the pizza stand?"

As the two walked back to the shack, a feeling of foreboding came over Nick. "Ritchie," he said, "take an ATV and circle the parade. Make sure there's nobody out there."

Ritchie put his hands up in protest. "Wait a minute, Nick," he said. "I was the guy who found Mr. Allison, remember? If there are any more stiffs out there, I sure don't want to be the one who finds them."

"You wanted to work today, right?" Nick asked.

"Full eight hours? You bet I do."

"Then take the ride, come back here, and I'll give you the keys to the shack."

Ritchie immediately took off for the garage. Nick had never turned the keys over to anyone, at least as far as he knew and if this was his chance to become Nick's assistant, he certainly wasn't going to blow it.

He was out on the ice for about five minutes, driving slowly, inspecting the rows. Everything was normal.

When Ritchie returned and reported all was well, Nick handed him the keys and told him he was taking the day off.

Wow! Now there's a first, Ritchie thought. Nick taking a day off. But the unusualness of the situation made him leery. "What's going on, Nick?" he asked.

"I'm sick, kid," came the reply. "I'm just sick of the whole damn thing."

26

At a quarter past eleven, Josh collected Winks and the two boys headed off to the lake. After finding a space in the parking lot, Josh and Winks followed the crowd out on the ice and nudged their way through to the Lead Snowman.

Sandwiched in among a crowd of about ten people, they inspected their creation. "Doesn't look any different from the other day," Winks said.

Josh agreed. "No, it doesn't."

Winks adjusted his watch cap and looked around. "Boy, this place is filling up fast. What is this, a holiday weekend or something?"

"Monday's Christmas, remember?" Josh said searching the area for any sign of Nick.

"Oh that's right!" Winks bumped the heel of his hand off his forehead in that "Boy am I a dope!" gesture.

Josh wasn't paying attention. He was still checking the crowd.

Winks turned back to the snowman and momentarily considered removing the hat and scarf himself. That would be pretty gutsy, he thought. The problem was, people were still taking pictures and such an act was bound to bring trouble.

Maybe tonight, after it's dark and the crowds are gone.

Just as that thought was running through his head, he watched in awe as Josh stepped up to the snowman, reached up and pulled off the hat, threw it to the ground and then started unwrapping the scarf. The crowd protested but Josh ignored them. He had almost finished when two hands dropped rather firmly on his shoulders.

"Young dude!" the voice said. "You know the rules."

Josh turned and saw Ritchie Parker staring down at him.

"Look, Ritchie," he said pulling free, "I've got to get this stuff off the snowman, I'll pay for a new hat and scarf."

"Let's step into my office," Ritchie said as he picked up the hat, placed it back on the snowman, and rewrapped the scarf. He motioned to Josh and they both walked over to the shack. Winks stayed right behind them silently cursing himself for not having the courage to do what Josh had just done.

Ritchie unlocked the door and they all went in. He pointed at two chairs and told the boys to sit down.

Ritchie opened his jacket and took a seat on the cot. "Okay," he said, "what's the deal?"

"No deal," Josh started to say but Winks quickly jumped in.

"It was my idea, Ritchie," he said. "That hat and scarf belong to Lucas Walks and unless we get them off that snowman more people are going to die."

Ritchie smiled thinking it was a joke. But after seeing the boys weren't smiling back it quickly dropped from his face. "What, you're serious? C'mon, don't jerk me around."

"We're not jerking you around, Ritchie," Winks protested. "Ever since me and Josh took those things out of his attic and put them on the snowman, people have been dying."

Ritchie shook his head. "Wait a minute, how can an old hat

and scarf have anything to do with people dying?"

"Because they belonged to Lucas Walks, that's why!" Winks said adamantly.

"Yeah, whatever, and who is this Lucas Walks?"

Josh picked it up from that point. "Walks was a murderer who was hanged thirty years ago. His body disappeared into the lake before they could bury him."

Ritchie folded his arms across his chest. "So you two think that because that hat and scarf belonged to this Walks guy, your grandfather and old man Allison are dead? Man, that's nuts! Anyway, you guys," he continued, leaning back against the wall, "I don't really care why you were trying to grab that stuff. Maybe one of your friends dared you. So go back and tell them that you tried, got busted and that I told you if I caught anybody trying that stunt again, I'd kick their ass. This way you look like a hero. All right?"

"But, Ritchie!" Winks protested.

"Listen, shorty," Ritchie replied sitting up. "Nick went home sick today and left me in charge. And the last thing I need is for him to come back and see that some dopey kids vandalized the Lead Snowman. Comprendo? So take your ghost stories and get out of here."

"Ritchie," Josh said. "We're serious and we need your help."

Ritchie saw the earnestness in Josh's face. He studied it for a moment then hung his head down and let out a deep sigh. "Look guys, you two are old enough to know why you can't change the Lead Snowman's look. See those flatlanders out there?" he said pointing to the window. "I guarantee that half of them have a picture from their hometown newspaper of the parade. They drive all the way up here just so they can have their picture taken with the Lead Snowman. So what do you think is going to happen if we start screwing around with it?"

Both Josh and Winks were silent.

"So you see my point. But hey, I'm not unreasonable. Maybe we can work something out. I'll tell you what. If you can get a hat and scarf that look enough like the ones on it now, I'll look the other way when you make the switch. Fair enough?"

"But where are we supposed to get them?" Josh asked.

"That's your problem, dude. That's my best offer."

"All right," Winks said. "Me and Josh will look around."

"Good," the Parker boy replied as he climbed off the cot. "Oh, and don't let me catch you trying that again. Got it?"

"Got it," Josh said sullenly as he climbed out of the chair.

Both he and Winks were almost out the door when Ritchie's curiosity got the better of him.

"Hey, you said if you don't get rid of the hat and scarf, more people are going to die. Like who?"

"Like my dad and Mr. McKay!" Winks said without thinking.

The reply startled Ritchie. "Theo McKay?" he said. "Weird!"

Josh stopped at the door. "What's so weird about that?"

Ritchie zipped up his jacket and joined them. "It's probably nothing, but me and Nick found McKay's car abandoned with the motor running behind the pizza stand this morning."

"Has anybody seen him since?" Josh asked.

"Well, I haven't," Ritchie replied. "But I'm sure he's all right."

But as the boys walked off, Ritchie realized that he wasn't so sure after all.

"All right, so what do we do now?" Josh asked as they climbed aboard the snowmobile.

"Try the Salvation Army I guess. But first, let's stop at my house. I forgot to feed Jean-Paul this morning. And I think I should tell my dad about Theo McKay."

Josh nodded and they drove off.

The two boys entered the Shays home and went directly to Winks' room.

"Is your dad home?" Josh asked as he closed the door behind them.

"I saw his truck outside, but I'm not sure. If we're lucky he's out with Mr. McKay. I'll check to see if he's here right after I feed Jean-Paul."

The first thing that caught their attention was that Jean-Paul wasn't on his perch. In fact, it looked like he wasn't in the cage at all. That morning, when Winks took off the cover, Jean-Paul seemed fine. Winks had intended to feed him but it slipped his mind when Josh showed up to take him to the lake.

"Jean-Paul?" Winks called, approaching the cage. There was no answer.

"Jean-Paul?" he said again, only this time he was close enough to see that his parrot was lying on the floor of the cage, awake but obviously sick.

"Oh man!" Winks rushed out to the hall praying that his father was in the house. "Dad! Dad!" he shouted.

Mike Shays walked in from the kitchen and stood at the bottom of the stairs. "What's the matter?"

"Dad, it's Jean-Paul. I think he's sick."

Mike quickly climbed the stairs, entered the room, and went directly to the cage. "Jean-Paul? Jean-Paul?" he said but when the bird didn't respond, he opened the door, reached in and petted the bird's wing. Jean-Paul barely moved. Seeing the bird was ill, Mike instructed Winks to call the vet and ask if they could bring him right in.

"This is all my fault," he said running from the room to the telephone. "I should have fed him when I was supposed to."

Mike closed the door, unhooked the cage from the stand, and carefully inspected the bird. "I'm no vet," he said, "but this poor thing's in trouble."

"We'll go with you," Josh offered.

Mike shook his head. "I'd rather you didn't. Theodore is very attached to Jean-Paul and the boy's been edgy lately. It would be better if I took the bird and called you both here at the house. If it's nothing, I'll bring him right home. If it's serious, then you two can come down."

Josh didn't think that idea was going to sit well with his friend but he knew from Winks' stories that once Mike Shays had made up his mind, arguing was a waste of time.

The vet had given the okay to bring him in and Mike had taken the bird and gone outside to warm up the truck. As Josh had suspected, Winks didn't like the idea of waiting at the house one bit but did as he was told.

"This sucks!" Winks said throwing himself down on his bed. "He still thinks I'm a little kid. I'm not you know, I can handle it."

Josh grasped the birdcage stand, looked out the window, and saw Mike drive off.

"Well, your dad's on his way. Nothing you can do now."

"Do you think Jean-Paul will be all right?" Winks asked sitting up.

More than anything Josh wanted to say "Sure! He'll be fine," but didn't. Josh always hated it when adults said that to kids when they knew the exact opposite was true. He refused to treat his friend like a child.

"I don't know, Winks," he said finally. "I really hope he will be."

Winks nodded. "Me too."

27

In order to get to the veterinarian Mike had to drive along Shore Road. He had the heat on and Jean-Paul in his cage on the seat beside him. As he neared the entrance to the Snowman's Parade, he slowed with the traffic. There was a lot of stop and go driving in that area until you got by the parking lots and concession stands. During one of those stops he looked out the window and saw the crowds surrounding the Lead Snowman. Staring in anger, Mike found himself talking aloud.

"Keep smiling you SOB. Tomorrow night Theo and I are going to take care of you once and for all."

He had just shifted back into gear when he heard a strange voice. "Mikeeey," it said.

Startled, Mike looked around the inside of the truck to find the source. Seeing nothing, he checked the radio. It was off. Then he looked at the cage.

Jean-Paul was slowly climbing back on his perch, rocking his head from side to side. It was as if he was listening to some strange music only he could hear.

The traffic had begun to move and Mike inched along with it. There was silence for the next few moments, then....

"I have friends. Powerful friends."

Mike's jaw fell slack. It was the parrot. Its eyes had rolled back up into its head. Only the whites were visible. Its body began to shake as if it had some kind of palsy.

A horn blared. Mike jumped, saw that he had fallen behind the cars in front of him and hurried to catch up.

As he drove, the parrot continued to speak. "From the deepest pit in hell, Mikey," it said.

Although Mike could see it was the parrot speaking, he couldn't understand how the bird could know those words or who could have taught them to him. He looked around again for some sort of speaker or tape recorder, momentarily lost sight of the road, jumped the curb, and knocked over a trash barrel. Horns again blared and pedestrians gave the truck a wide berth. Mike steeled himself and turned his attention back to his driving.

"What's going on here?!" he shouted, eyes glued to the road.

"Mikey…Mikey…Mikey!" the bird said. It was bouncing up and down and its head was jerking as if it was being electrocuted. Yet it held on to the perch as if it were nailed there.

"Mikey, Mikey, Mikeeeey!!!" it shrieked. "I will have my revenge on all of you!"

Perspiration ran down Mike's face in torrents. He wanted to reach out, grab the bird, and snap its neck. But it was his son's pet. How could he ever explain that to the boy?

The traffic stopped again. He was still in front of the parade. He looked out and saw two tourists having their picture taken with the Lead Snowman.

"Ernie, dead! Morris, dead! And Theeeooooo…," it squealed. "DEAD!!!!"

"You son of a bitch!" Mike howled and flung open the door of the truck. By taking his foot off the clutch the engine stalled immediately.

"FUHH...FUHHH...FUHHH...YEH...YEH...YEW!!!
MIKEY!!!!" The bird screeched and then fell over dead.

Mike hadn't seen the bird die. He was already running across
Shore Road to the Snowman's Parade.

Theo can't be dead. He can't!!

Mike pushed past tourists and shoved those who didn't move
fast enough. Amid shouts and threats, Mike ran straight for the
tool shed and kicked the door open.

He emerged from it with a pickax slung over his shoulder and
started running toward the Lead Snowman as quickly as the icy
surface would allow.

Theo can't be dead. He just can't be.

People screamed and pointed as Mike barreled toward them.
Seeing what they thought was a madman wielding a pickax, everyone dropped what they were doing and ran for safety.

Hearing all the commotion, Ritchie Parker climbed out of the
ice shack and saw Mike charging toward the Lead Snowman with
the pick. "Dude!" he shouted. "Don't do it!!"

But Mike was obsessed, nothing was going to stop him. He
was going to end it, now!

Mike skidded across the last few feet of ice before reaching the
snowman. While still in motion he slammed the pickax straight in
to the center of the snowman's chest. He yanked it out and hit it
again. He pulled back for a third strike when a woman screamed.

"There's blood! There's blood!" she shouted.

Momentarily startled, Mike stopped and stood back. As he
did, he saw a crimson trail running down the front of the snowman. Mike dropped the pickax and, as it clattered against the ice,
the torso and bottom part of the snowman cracked and burst open.
From it fell the body of Theo McKay.

28

"Yes, this is Theodore Shays," Winks said. "Who's calling?"

It had been two hours since Mike had left and they had both jumped when the phone rang. Winks grabbed it and Josh stood beside his friend with his fingers crossed hoping that the news on Jean-Paul would be good.

"My father is where?!!" Winks face turned white and his hand began to shake as he held the phone. Josh uncrossed his fingers and slid his hand into his pocket for the snowmobile's keys. He had a feeling they were going to be leaving as soon as Winks put down the receiver.

"Yes, I know where it is…. Yes, I'll bring the checkbook. Okay…I'm leaving now. Good-bye."

Josh immediately grabbed their coats from the radiator.

"Where are we going?" Josh asked.

Winks put his hand to his head as he put down the phone.

"Winks, where are we going?" Josh asked a little more firmly this time.

The harshness of Josh's tone snapped Winks out of it. "The Municipal Center, my father's in jail."

Josh was shocked. "In jail? Why?"

Winks shook his head. "I'm not sure."

"Who was that on the phone?" Josh asked, handing Winks his coat.

"Mr. Ledbetter. He says he's an attorney. He told me to come right away."

"Winks what…what's going on? I thought your father was taking Jean-Paul to the vet."

"I don't know," Winks said as he slipped on his coat. "He said something about an accident down by the lake. The truck had to be towed. My father has to see the judge and…."

Winks legs started to wobble and he almost fell. Josh reached over and grabbed his arm. "Easy, pal," he said.

The Municipal Center was a brightly lit steel and glass structure with dark one-way windows, a large parking lot, and a giant radio tower situated just west of the main entrance.

When Josh and Winks arrived, they were met at the door by Sheriff Parker. The sheriff escorted them through the building and down the hall to the area marked Judicial/Detention.

As they walked, Parker assured Winks that his father was unharmed, the truck undamaged, and that there was no reason to be alarmed. "I'm sure everything will be straightened out by this evening," he said. Winks tried to press him for information but Parker explained that he was not permitted to comment on the case.

"All your questions will be answered by Mr. Ledbetter," he said.

Judicial/Detention was in the basement and after following the ramp down, they were met by two guards who opened the steel door and let them in. Once inside they were greeted by a tall balding man carrying a briefcase. He spoke briefly with the sheriff and then turned to Winks.

"Theodore, my name is Murray Ledbetter," the man said extending his hand. "I have been retained to represent your father in this matter. He's very anxious to see you so if you'll just follow me." Winks began to speak but Ledbetter cut him off. "I know you must have a million questions," he said opening and then removing some papers from his briefcase, "but I must ask that you wait until we meet with your father before asking them." Then he turned to Josh. "Excuse me," he said. "Are you a member of the family?"

"Josh is my best friend," Winks replied. "I want him to come with me."

Ledbetter closed the valise and shook his head. "I'm sorry but that's not possible. Josh if you would please sit over there in the waiting area," he said motioning to a row of chairs against the wall, "Theodore will be back just as soon as we finish."

Josh bristled at Ledbetter's condescending attitude but knew that there wasn't much he could do about it, so he took a seat and waited.

It was over an hour before Winks returned. He looked sick and drawn. His eyes were red from crying and his face was the color of a wet sweat sock. Ledbetter was still with him. The lawyer, as usual, was all business and displayed the emotions of a tombstone.

"Mr. Shays will be appearing before Judge Rand later this evening," he told Josh. "At that time I will request that bail be set and he be released. Whether he is or not is entirely up to the judge. Theodore tells me that he can stay with your family until that matter is resolved. If not he will have to be remanded to family services since he has no other relatives in the area."

"Yes, yes!" Josh replied, appalled at the idea of Winks being shunted off to a group home. "He can definitely stay with us."

Ledbetter's face remained stoic and cold. "The sheriff is calling your parents. If he gets their approval, Theodore can go home with you now."

They stood around in silence until the sheriff came out and announced that Roy Campbell had agreed to take Winks in until Mike was released.

"Stay where we can reach you, Theodore," Ledbetter said. "I'm sure that when your father gets out he'll want to get in touch with you right away."

"We'll stay at my house," Josh said taking Winks by the arm and leading him to the exit.

29

When they reached Josh's house they found Roy Campbell outside spreading rock salt and breaking up ice on the walkway. He smiled when he saw the boys approach and pointed to the open garage. Josh understood that to mean that he wanted them to park the snowmobile in there and to go directly into the house.

Josh pulled in, shut down the machine and the two boys entered through the connecting door. As they peeled off their gear, the smell of food cooking in the kitchen eased Winks back to the real world. The last few hours had been his personal journey into hell and he was relieved to be back in a place that housed the welcomed sights and smells of normal life.

The boys followed their noses and discovered that Marion was waiting for them in the kitchen with some hot soup and sandwiches. Winks, still recovering from shock, simply nodded to Josh's mom and following his friend's lead, pulled out one of the red upholstered chairs from the kitchen table and sat down.

Winks didn't particularly feel like eating but the aroma of the vegetable soup and the warmth it gave off set his stomach rumbling. He picked up his spoon from the gingham tablecloth, dipped it into the soup bowl, and began to stir.

"Hellooo!" Roy called out from the mud porch as he kicked the snow off his boots.

"We're in here, dear," Marion replied from the kitchen. Roy nodded and headed down the hall to join the rest of the family. As he entered the room, the first thing he noticed was Winks' forlorn expression. Seeing this, Roy dropped his coat on the back of the chair and sat down next to him.

"Hi, Theodore," he said. "How are you holding up?"

"Okay, I guess," Winks muttered.

"I spoke with Sheriff Parker and from what I understand, both he and Mr. Ledbetter are confident your father will be released this evening."

Winks looked up and Roy was instantly touched by the sadness in the young boy's eyes. He felt terrible at having to tell him of the other possibility. "However…," he continued, "sometimes the courts work slowly and things are delayed. So, just in case a problem arises, I want you to know that you're welcome to stay here indefinitely."

"That means as long as you like, Theodore," Marion quickly added.

Winks put down the spoon and rubbed his eyes and nose with the sleeve of his shirt. "I just want to go home," he said.

Roy patted Winks on the back sympathetically. "I know."

Seeing that there was nothing more they could do to improve Winks' mood, Roy and Marion left the room.

Josh eyed his friend. He knew he had to be careful about what he asked, especially when Winks was so upset. But damn! How could he help if he didn't know what was going on?

"I can't tell you anything," Winks said as if reading Josh's mind. "Mr. Ledbetter said so. He said if I did, you might be asked to repeat it in court. This is bad enough, Josh, I don't want to drag you into it."

Josh reached for his sandwich. "I'm already dragged into it, pal."

Winks was startled. "What do you mean?"

"What I mean is we both built the snowman. Both of us, got that? So stop playing the strong silent type and tell me what you know."

"But Mr. Ledbetter...."

"Screw Mr. Ledbetter!" Josh said angrily but not loud enough for his parents to hear. "Theo McKay disappeared this morning and if we don't get to the bottom of this thing soon they might find him dead, too."

Winks put his face in his hands. "Theo McKay IS dead."

"What!!??"

Winks took a deep breath as tears began to well up in his eyes. "That's why my father is in jail. When he was driving down Shore Road, he suddenly stopped the truck in the middle of traffic, ran over to the tool shed, got a pickax, and slammed it through the center of the Lead Snowman. Mr. Ledbetter says eyewitnesses claim he hit it two or three times."

A look of confusion came over Josh's face. "You mean that's it? Your father is in jail for trashing the Lead Snowman? I don't get it, Winks, as far as I know that's not even a crime. I mean he might have to pay a fine or something...."

Winks looked over at Josh angrily. "Who cares about the stupid snowman! After my father hit it with the pickax, Mr. McKay's body fell out with two holes in his chest! And if that isn't bad enough, Mr. Ledbetter said that the police were reopening the case on your grandfather and Mr. Allison. He says the prosecution believes that he may be responsible for their deaths as well."

Josh's eyes widened. He couldn't speak.

"Jean-Paul is dead too," he said sadly. "I saw them bringing in his cage when I was at the Municipal center. I ran over to it before anyone could stop me." Although he tried desperately to control it, tears were rolling down Winks' face. "He was lying at the bottom of the cage, Josh, blood was running from his eyes. He was dead but the blood...the blood...."

Winks bowed his head into his arms and blubbered uncontrollably.

Josh sat back in his chair. This was simply too much. Had the man who actually hanged a serial killer become one himself? Did Winks' dad kill his grandfather, Mr. Allison, and Theo McKay? No, he just couldn't believe that, but what was the other option, a killer snowman?

But if Michael Shays killed those three people, why would he leave their bodies to be found? And why would he take a pick ax and smash the Lead Snowman when he knew Theo McKay's body was in it? It didn't make any sense.

He had to know more. He decided that before he got further involved he'd better be sure Mike Shays wasn't the real killer and that Winks hadn't been lying to him all along.

Josh tapped Winks on the arm.

Winks looked up. His eyes were red and tear-stained. "What?"

"What's really going on?"

"I don't understand," Winks replied somewhat confused.

"About your father," Josh said coldly. "I want to know the truth, are you covering up for him?"

Winks bolted upright. "How could you ask such a thing? My father's the nicest guy anywhere. He'd never hurt anyone. I'm sure of it."

Josh stared at him. "We both know that isn't true."

Winks' face turned ashen. He again buried his face in his hands and began crying all the more.

Josh had had enough. He reached out, grabbed Winks by the front of his shirt, and yanked the smaller boy toward him. "Listen to me," he said sharply. "My grandfather's dead, Mr. Allison is dead, and now Theo McKay is dead. Good people are dead, Winks, and your father is a suspect. So enough of this crying. I want to know, did he do it?"

Josh's coldness and aggressive behavior was like a slap in the face. Josh was his hero. How could he treat him this way?

Winks pulled out of Josh's grasp. "No! He didn't!" Winks shouted.

"How can you be sure?" Josh fired back.

"Because I was home with him the night your grandfather died," Winks blubbered.

"Are you sure or are you just saying that to protect your father?"

"I'm saying it because it's true and if you don't believe me you can go to hell!!"

Josh waited for his parents to come charging in. They didn't.

When he turned back, his friend had a question for him.

"Why are you treating me like this? You're worse than Billy Curtis," Winks said wiping his eyes.

"Because a crying person is a useless person," Josh replied and regretted the words the moment they left his mouth. Realizing that he had been too harsh, and remembering that Michael Shays would have no way of knowing that his grandfather would show up at the lake when he did, he bit down on his lip and made a decision. Winks was telling the truth.

"I'm sorry," Josh said sincerely. "That was way too rough. It's just that all this is making me crazy. We've got to do something to stop it."

"We can't do anything, Josh," Winks replied in a teary voice. "We're only kids."

He then put his head in his hands and went silent.

Josh didn't want to press Winks any further seeing that the boy was on the verge of falling apart, but he knew Winks was wrong. There was always something you could do, but the problem was getting Winks to believe that. He returned to his meal and as he ate came upon something he was sure would convince his friend all was not lost.

Josh finished up and pushed the empty bowl aside. "Remember the time you told me about the superheroes and how they always stood up to bullies even if they didn't have super powers?" he asked.

"Yeah..." Winks replied keeping his head buried.

"Well, during my grandfather's wake, we would stand around outside the viewing room for hours with nothing to do. That got boring so I started going outside for air. Anyway, I'm walking around and I notice that across the street is that comic book store you're always going on about. So I went over to take a look. Since I don't know one superhero from another I asked the guy what he would recommend. He brought back this comic called *Origins*."

"I know the one you mean," Winks said looking up.

Josh nodded. "So I bought it, just to kill time, you know? Well, I got to admit, it was pretty good. Especially the origin of Spider-Man."

A slight smile came over Winks face. Spider-Man was one of his favorites.

"It was sad the way Spider-Man felt he was responsible for his Uncle Ben's death."

"I know," Winks said, "I felt bad for him, too."

"Yeah, but remember, Winks, Spider-Man went after the guy who killed his uncle. Single-handedly brought him to justice. And remember, he was just a kid too."

Winks sat up straight and thought for a moment. "That's right!" he replied. "His uncle died because Spider-Man didn't stop the burglar when he had the chance." Winks mind was racing and he was beginning to see the point Josh was trying to make. Super powers or not, it wasn't too late for him to save his dad!

Winks looked as if a weight had suddenly been removed from his back. He nodded gently at first and then enthusiastically. He returned to his food while continuing to shake his head up and down.

"You're right, Josh!" he said after swallowing several spoonfuls of soup. "It's not too late. You know, I'll bet my father knew that Walks killed your grandfather and Morris Allison and that's why he went nuts and bashed the snowman and that's why...." Winks stopped for a second. "Wait, I just remembered," he said dropping the spoon into the bowl, "after Mr. Ledbetter told me why my father had been arrested, I asked him what happened to the snowman's hat and scarf. I'm not even sure why I asked, but I did. Well, he gave me this strange look and then told me that my father had asked him the same thing. He said he wanted to know what made them so important but I was too freaked out to answer. Anyway, I guess he felt sorry for me so he told me that while the EMS people were removing Mr. McKay's body, a gust of wind blew the hat and scarf away. He said they searched for a while because there might be blood evidence on them but they were gone."

"Damn!" Josh said. "Do you think that now that he's gotten

his revenge, Walks will disappear?"

Winks shook his head. "I don't think so."

"Why not?"

"Because my father's still alive. If my father was in on Walks' hanging, I don't think he'll stop until my dad is dead. The hat and scarf are out there somewhere and we've got to find them."

Josh leaned in. "Okay, but we've got two problems. First, my parents aren't going to let us out of their sight until they hear from your father. Second, after what happened this afternoon, the parade is probably going to be roped off again."

As scared as he was, he knew that if he was to have any chance at saving his father's life, he had to act now. But how were they going to get past the police barriers? Then it hit him. "Christmas!" Winks said suddenly.

"What about it?"

"Monday is Christmas, Josh," Winks replied "The weekend before Christmas is always the biggest. The town will be flooded with people. I'll bet the "Crime Scene" tape and police barriers have already been taken down."

Josh lit up. "I'll bet you're right."

Winks started to plan. "Maybe we can sneak out later tonight and go down there."

"No," Josh replied shaking his head, "that's another problem. The only way to get down to the parade is to use the snowmobile. If I fire that up in the middle of the night my parents will be on us before we leave the driveway. Maybe early tomorrow morning."

"It has to be tonight, Josh," Winks said coldly.

"Why?"

"Gut feeling."

Josh held up his hand and turned when he thought he heard

the sound of a door close out in the hall. But after waiting a moment and hearing no one approach, he let Winks continue.

"When I was with my dad at the jail, I remembered your talk with your grandfather. My dad is just like him. He's not going to stop until he makes things right." Winks eyes started tearing up again. "And I'll bet Walks knows it too! He's going to wait until my father comes to the parade and he's going to kill him there. That way my father will never be able to prove he's innocent and everyone will believe that he was responsible for the deaths of your grandfather, Mr. Allison, and Mr. McKay."

The boys heard footsteps approach the kitchen door. It was Marion.

"Well, boys, are you still hungry?" she asked poking her head in. Both Josh and Winks said they were not.

"Well, then, why don't you strong fellows give me a hand lugging in some wood. It's starting to get cold in here and I think it's time to fire up the stove."

"Sure, Mom," Josh said rising from his chair. "But where's dad?"

"Your father got a call on his cell," she replied as she gathered the dishes from the table and brought them to the sink. "As usual, some people wait until they're completely out of fuel and then plead for an emergency delivery. He shouldn't be more than a couple of hours."

Winks looked out the kitchen window. It was already getting dark.

They all brought in wood for the stove and Marion let Josh do the honors of lighting it. When he put his hand on the mantle to get the fireplace matches he discovered the box was empty.

"Mom, we're out of matches."

Marion shook her head. "Ohhhhh! I was going to pick them

up on my way home from work and it slipped my mind."

Josh crushed the empty box and headed for the kitchen. "Well, I can get a light from the kitchen stove. I'll just roll up a paper plate and…."

"Hold it right there, Josh," Marion said stopping the boy in his tracks, "I don't want you carrying a flaming piece of cardboard through the house. Now there's got to be matches around here somewhere," she said. "Maybe in one of the cupboards."

Josh and Marion, with Winks in tow, began searching the cupboards but with no success. Winks decided to check the living room again and saw Roy's Zippo lighter lying on the end table. "Mrs. Campbell," he called out, "does this lighter work?"

Marion came in and was surprised to see that Roy had left the Zippo behind. "Oh, good," she said. "Roy was probably in such a rush he forgot to take it with him."

Josh picked it up and gave the wheel a spin. "Hey, it works!"

"Of course," Marion replied. "He takes very good care of it."

Josh took the lighter over to the woodburning stove and opened the door. After opening the flue, he took out a firestarter brick and carefully lit both ends. He placed it in the stove, loaded a few pieces of wood on top of it, then closed the door. Josh then slipped the lighter into his pocket so he would have it handy in case the fire went out.

Time seemed to drag and both boys were getting anxious. They needed to get down to the lake, but with Marion hovering about, escape was impossible.

Finally, the phone rang. Josh's mom picked it up and after the first few sentences were exchanged, they knew it was Mike Shays on the line.

"Here," she said handing the phone over to Winks, "your father would like to speak to you."

Winks smiled, took the phone, and watched as Josh and Marion left the room.

"When are you getting out?" Winks asked.

"It might be awhile yet, son. The autopsy was just completed on poor Theo, and the judge, the prosecutor, and my lawyer are hammering out the details. It turns out that Theo had been dead long before I got to the lake so it looks like they'll be dropping the charges at least for the time being. However, the prosecutor is still trying to convince the judge that I had something to do with Ernie Campbell's and Morris Allison's deaths, which is complete nonsense. My lawyer says he hasn't a leg to stand on but it's probably going to take some more time before I'm released, so...."

"I understand," Winks replied.

"Anyway, if this thing drags on you might have to stay the night. Are you okay with that?"

"Sure, they've been very nice."

"Glad to hear it. Now you hang tough, son, and I'll be home before you know it. Now put Mrs. Campbell back on the line. I want to thank her again and make sure we're not inconveniencing them."

Winks knew that if he did as he was told he'd never get out to the lake before his father did. Summoning up his courage, he decided now was the time to make his move.

"You just missed her," he lied. "She left for the Mini-mart to pick up some milk. But she already told me that I can stay."

"Oh that's great. Thank her for me and I'll call back if I get out of here before your bedtime. Otherwise, I'll pick you up in the morning. Okay?"

"You bet, dad. I'll see you later." Winks put down the receiver and walked into the kitchen where Marion and Josh were sitting at the table.

"My father's just been released and is on his way home now," Winks announced. "It turns out Mr. McKay died last night, not this afternoon…."

"I just knew this was a terrible mix up," she said. "Still, it's a shame about poor Theo. How about we have some hot chocolate while we wait for your father?"

"Thanks, Mrs. Campbell," Winks replied. "But he asked me to meet him at the house. He sounded real tired so I'd better get going. I want to turn on the heat and make my dad some dinner. He's had a real rough day."

"Fine," Marion said rising from the table. "I'll get my coat and warm up the van."

Winks glared at Josh with a look that told him to stop her. Josh got the hint.

"Oh, Mom," Josh said. "I'll take Winks home in the snowmobile. He'll probably need to bring in some wood and I wanted to borrow one of his CD's."

Marion eyed her son. "Josh, it's late and you know I don't like you driving that thing around after dark."

"Oh c'mon, Mom," Josh pleaded. "It's only next door. I could be there and back before you got the van warmed up."

Like every mother, Marion had her own "gut feeling" and wondered if the boys were being completely honest with her. Probably not, she figured, but suspected that was because Winks was embarrassed by having to be taken in and didn't want to impose any further. Besides, if she did drive them home she probably would have to wait around in the minivan while they brought in the wood and searched through the CD's. A half an hour at least she figured. She took a quick glance at her watch. Roy would be home soon and he'd probably be hungry. All in all it would be a lot easier if she let Josh do it. Reluctantly, she agreed.

"All right," she said. "But make it quick."

"Will do."

The boys suited up and ran out to the garage.

Winks noticed an old knapsack hanging on the wall. "We'd better bring some supplies," he said. "Finding the hat and scarf in the dark isn't going to be easy."

Josh agreed and together they stuffed the canvas bag with everything they thought might come in handy.

"Well, we're free," Josh said as he climbed on the snowmobile and put the key in the ignition. "What's the real story?"

"My dad says he won't be out for a couple of hours," Winks replied, slinging the knapsack over his back. "If we're ever going to do this, it's got to be now."

Josh put on his goggles and tossed a pair to Winks. He nodded, started the engine, and revved it a couple of times. "Okay, partner, let's ride!"

30

Like it had been shot out of a cannon, the snowmobile flew out of the garage and quickly turned down the road toward Winks' house. When they were sure they could no longer be seen, Josh made another turn. This time into the hills and toward the lake.

With it's single headlight piercing the darkness, the snowmobile rocketed over the snow-covered countryside and headed toward the far end of Morris Allison's property. It was there the estate grounds jutted out into the lake and served as a catchall for debris blown across the surface. They figured that would be the best place to begin their search.

"When we find the hat and scarf, we'll grab them, burn them, and leave before anyone knows we were there," Josh said.

Winks nodded but didn't agree. Inside, his gut feeling was shrieking louder than a cartoon air raid siren.

No Josh, no matter what you might think, this isn't going to be easy.

To keep his mind off the danger, Winks double-checked the knapsack. In it was a small hand ax, a pair of binoculars, and two flashlights. The supplies now seemed ridiculously inadequate when he remembered that three grown men had already attempted what they were setting out to do and had failed. But it was too late to turn back and with the minutes ticking away before Mike Shays' arrival, it would have to be enough.

As the snowmobile proceeded toward the Allison estate, they plowed over snow banks, snaked around trees, and plummeted down steep inclines. The wind seared the boys' faces and Josh's down jacket flapped against his body. And as the dark hulk of the Allison estate loomed before them, so did the realization that the endgame was about to begin.

Nick Pederuco was feeling particularly melancholy that evening. He sat in the ice shack with a cup of hot coffee cradled in his hands. It wasn't only coffee, however, along with it was a generous dose of scotch. And it wasn't his first cup.

Nick took a swig and then sucked on his teeth. Feeling the warmth run through him, he reached down, grabbed the bottle, and poured in a little more.

Poetic justice! That's what it is. That I should be here now, to see the results of my own stupidity. What on earth had I been thinking all these years? That I alone could control the lake? That I could keep it from feeding? The lake must have its sacrifices! It must. What a fool I've been!

He knew that now. The voices had explained it to him. The voices had made it all so very clear.

The voices.

The voices from *beneath* the ice.

"Almost made it, Pederuco," he said in a brief moment of clarity. "Almost."

He had tried to get out. When he left Ritchie Parker in charge, he had every intention of dropping off his resignation at the Municipal Center that afternoon and going on a long vacation. But he delayed, waiting to see whether or not Ritchie could handle the job. Well, unfortunately, he couldn't. After Theo McKay's body fell from the Lead Snowman, Ritchie took off like the devil himself was chasing him.

He really couldn't blame the kid. First he finds Morris Allison's head embedded in the ice and then Theo's dead body drops out in front of him with a fine howdoyoudo. Nick had to admit that if he were eighteen he probably would have beat it out of there just as quickly.

But now here he was, suckered back to his post, with calmer and more rational heads having prevailed.

Right after the incident, the Parade Committee called Nick and insisted that he return to work immediately. He tried to beg off. He was sick, he told them, tired, and wanted out. But they persisted. What about your responsibility to the community? Have you forgotten that the entire county depends on the parade? What about loyalty? Sparks would surely fall into bankruptcy. Surely you wouldn't let that happen.

No, no he couldn't do that.

So, against his better judgment he gave in and drove over to the ice shack for what was to be his last weekend on the lake. Next week the Committee had promised to hire a professional security force to guard the parade day and night.

"Day and night my ass!" Nick had said on the ride over. "They'll have some poor old retiree wandering around with a Radio Shack walkie-talkie freezing his butt off for minimum wage. That's their idea of a professional security force."

It had begun snowing outside but Nick was too wrapped up in his own thoughts to notice. His goals were simple enough now. He was going to sit quietly and make it through the rest of the weekend without any further trouble. The voices told him that if he did as he was told, everything would return to normal. "Normal!" he said laughing as he spilled some of the coffee/scotch on his hand. "Normal," he repeated only a lot darker this time, "ain't that a hoot."

He walked over and looked out the window. "Hmmm, snowing again!" he said aloud. He scanned the Shore Road and the empty concession stands, the tool shed, the pier, and then finally the parade.

In front was the Lead Snowman, it's head masked by the shadows from the speaker columns. Of course, it wasn't the same Lead Snowman. Upon his return, he had the crew sweep away the remains of the original and bring up a similar one to put in its place. It didn't look as good (the red ski cap it wore looked a little ratty and the scarf was such a pale gray that it was almost invisible) but it would do.

Nick walked back over to the chair and sat down. "Going to be a hot time in the old town tonight, Mikeeey," he said, unaware that he was speaking and then finished his drink.

If Nick had stayed at the window long enough for the moonlight to remove the shadows from the face of the Lead Snowman he would have seen what Josh and Winks were now seeing for themselves.

When they arrived at the inlet that cornered the Allison Estate, they began searching the bushes for the hat and scarf. For nearly twenty minutes they carefully combed the area. Unfortunately, they came up empty.

"Where could they have gone?" Josh said with mounting frustration.

Winks didn't answer. He had his flashlight glued to the surface, convinced that at any moment they were going to strike pay dirt. Then it had begun to snow.

"Oh, great!" Josh said. "If it keeps snowing we'll never find the hat and scarf. Any luck over there, Winks?"

Winks shook his head. He too was becoming frustrated but was determined to continue no matter how long it took or how difficult it became.

After several minutes Winks looked up. "Josh, we're going to have to move on. It doesn't seem to be here. Where do you want to try next?"

Josh folded his arms across his chest. "I don't know," he said. "I figured that if they were blown across the lake, they would probably wind up here. Now, your guess is as good as mine." Josh looked down the shore. "All right, hand me the binoculars, I'll check out the brush farther down and see if there's anything poking out."

Winks handed the binoculars over and Josh began his search. As he scanned the shoreline the moon slowly slid out from behind the snowy clouds and it's reflection illuminated the lake like it was a sheet of glass.

"Hey, Winks," he said. "the moon's working like a freakin' spotlight. Maybe our luck's about to change."

The words had no sooner left his lips when he happened to scan the front of the Snowman's Parade. What he saw caused his breath to hitch up in his chest. He pulled the binoculars from his eyes, rubbed them, and then looked again.

He hadn't been mistaken nor was he seeing things. The hat and scarf of Lucas Walks was again on the head and around the neck of the Lead Snowman!

Josh tossed the binoculars to Winks and ran over to start the snowmobile.

"What is it, Josh?" he asked. "What did you see?"

Receiving no answer, Winks brought up the binoculars and took a look for himself.

"Holy crap! Ritchie put the hat and scarf back on the snowman." Winks took a step back and thought for a moment as Josh revved the snowmobile's engine. "Wait a second! Josh, our snowman was destroyed. Mr. Ledbetter told me so himself."

Josh spun the snowmobile around and brought it over. Winks shook his head. "It can't be the same snowman, Josh."

"Yes it can, if it can strangle my grandfather, freeze old man Allison's head in the ice, and become a coffin for Mr. McKay, it can do just about anything."

"Wait a second," Winks said as he climbed on the seat, "somebody's in the ice shack. I can see a light."

"I saw it too," Josh replied slipping on his goggles, "But if we stay low and motor across Allison's property and use the trees and brush for cover, we can hit the ice at the back of the parade and stay behind the tarps until we reach the front. Then, we slam into the snowman, take the hat and scarf and boom! We're gone."

Winks had to admit he liked the sound of that. With the parade music playing over the loudspeakers there was little chance the snowmobile would be heard until it was too late.

Winks took a deep breath. "Okay, Josh," he shouted. "I'm ready!"

The boys took off and raced across Allison's property keeping their eyes on the lake from behind the snow-covered pines. As the trees whipped by, Winks looked up and noticed the moon was still quite visible in the sky. That struck him as odd because it was snowing and he wondered if it was a good omen or bad. He figured he'd find out as soon as they reached the lake.

Winks held tight as Josh made the turn down the hillside. As the lake drew nearer, their speed increased rapidly. It was at that point a strange feeling came over Josh. A feeling of lightheadedness and confusion. Another trick, Josh thought, as he angled the snow-mobile around the last few birch trees toward the ice. As he pressed forward, the snow began to swirl before him in an almost circular motion. He shook his head trying to clear it but the constant motion brought back the feeling of dizziness and disorientation. No matter how many times he blinked or wiped the snow from his goggles, the vortex continued to spin in front of him.

The white dots twinkled and soon began to resemble stars. Stars spinning in a black sky. They turned slowly, hypnotically. The surrounding area began to fade, then disappear. Josh felt as if he were sliding into a giant tunnel, deep in outer space, drifting, lost and out of control. Deeper and deeper he went until the stars were all around him.

Where am I? What am I doing?

The air around him felt cool and pleasant and no longer cold. The snowmobile was gone and instead he was sitting in his bed at home and in his room. Yes, that's where he was. It had all been a dream. A long and silly dream. He looked around and saw the wallpaper in his room had little snowmen on it. Smiling snowmen. "Time for bed, Josh," they seemed to be saying. Yes, he thought, he was tired and he was ready to go to sleep….

"Josh! Josh! For heaven's sake slow down!" Winks shouted and pounded on his friends back. The snowmobile was racing at top speed down the side of the hill that led to the ice. He had to slow down or they would hit the surface head on.

"Ohhhhh shiiiiiii…!" Winks screamed as they ricocheted off the ice. The snowmobile twisted and threw Winks into the air.

"Yahhhhhh!" he shouted as he free fell toward the surface.

Josh was still in the driver's seat when the snowmobile crashed, bounced, and rolled over on its side.

Winks landed butt first into a snowdrift that the DPW created when they did their morning plowing.

Josh wasn't so lucky. Although he avoided serious injury, the snowmobile came to rest on his leg. As his head began to clear, he reached down and felt it. It wasn't broken but he could tell it was severely bruised and already it was beginning to swell.

Winks ran over to Josh and helped pull him from under the snowmobile. As Josh staggered to his feet, a sharp pain knifed at his ankle.

"Oh, man!" he growled, gritting his teeth.

"Are you all right?" Winks asked almost panicking. "I was shouting my head off but you were completely out of it!"

Josh pulled down his partially broken goggles, rubbed his face, and stared off at the tall pines that surrounded the lake. They were swaying back and forth in the wind. For a moment it looked to him like they were mocking him. Laughing. "Ha ha, Mr. Tough Guy. The first round isn't even over and we already knocked you on your ass."

Josh turned away and looked at Winks. His small round face was wide and confused. "Are you okay, Josh?" he asked.

"The snowman messed with my head," he replied. "It made it so I didn't know where I was or what I was doing." Josh took a deep breath. "Winks, it knows we're here and it knows what we're planning to do."

Winks was starting to have trouble breathing. "Okay, okay," he said trying to calm himself. "We knew this wasn't going to be easy but at least we're still in one piece." Winks brushed the snow off the back of his pants and looked over at the snowmobile. The engine was silent and he could see the left rail had snapped off. "Well, so much for plan A," he said. "Looks like we're going to have to do this on foot."

Josh nodded and Winks trotted over to the snowmobile to pick up the bag. As he slung it over his shoulder he told himself over and over: Don't think about it! Don't think about anything but the hat and scarf. And then for some reason he said aloud, "You screw up boy and your old man dies. Yes sir!"

"What did you say?" Josh asked, thinking Winks was talking to him.

"Nothing, Josh," he said shaking his head. "Let's get this over with."

31

As the two boys trudged over the ice, the moon dipped behind the clouds and the area grew ominously dark. Using the spotlights on the speaker columns and the soft glow of the sodium-arc lamps on Shore Road to guide them, they pressed on toward the parade.

As they drew nearer, they noticed that in the dim lighting the snowmen began to look like the giant carved heads on Easter Island, and atop the surrounding hills the pine trees resembled rows of crosses and hangman's gallows.

"More tricks," they said almost in unison but the fact that they were only illusions didn't ward off their growing panic. They picked up the pace in spite of Josh's sore ankle.

When they reached the snowmen and began walking alongside them, the holiday music playing in the background started to slur and deteriorate. It was as if someone was replacing the instruments on the recordings with cheap plastic imitations.

The booming sound of the bass drum began sounding like someone kicking the bottom of a barn door. The rich texture of the horn section decayed into what sounded like cheap toy kazoos. The rat-a-tat of the snare drum resembled a pie pan being struck by a wooden spoon. The closer they came the more the time and tempo twisted until it sounded ethereal and unreal. It was as if someone was ridiculing the music by deliberately playing it out of tune.

Josh felt a chill run up his spine. He tried to remain confident but was beginning to wonder if they had bitten off more that they could chew.

Even though the light of the moon had returned, a grayness had enveloped the area. Huge snowdrifts were forming along the shoreline. The clouds, once white, were now darkening and increasing in size. The pines faded and disappeared into almost total blackness. The lake itself looked as barren as the moon.

Winks had said nothing up to this point but the sudden change did not go unnoticed. "Damn creepy," he said finally. Josh only nodded.

There were over twenty-five rows of snowmen, three to each row. The boys walked side by side and were nearly half way to the front when the wind picked up. Josh was blown backward and had to be steadied by Winks who almost fell over himself. Josh winced with the pain in his ankle but hunched up his shoulders and pressed on.

The snow momentarily turned into ice pellets and battered them like peas from a peashooter, and for several moments their eyes were tearing so badly neither could see. When the winds finally slowed and the ice turned back to snow, Josh backed up a foot or two to get his bearings.

There was something behind him!

Josh spun around, fists clenched, and saw one of the snowmen standing directly before him. It wasn't the Lead Snowman but another. This one wore a black derby, carried a plastic trumpet, and looked quite harmless. Josh let out a sigh of relief but then began to wonder.

"How did that get there?" he asked.

Winks' face was pale and his eyes betrayed the panic that was welling up inside him. He didn't answer Josh's question. "Let's keep moving," was all he said.

The boys continued but got no more than a few feet when out of the corner of their eyes they saw another snowman standing several yards to their right. This one had a bass drum and like the one with the derby didn't seem to pose any threat but still, how did it get out there and why wasn't it in line with the others?

Josh suddenly realized what was going on. "Run!" he shouted as he grabbed Winks shoulder. As they looked back, their eyes widened when they saw that the parade was thinning out! Where there had been snowmen, three abreast in row after row, there were now only one or two.

Acting instinctively, they hobbled toward the center of the lake. Josh's ankle jabbed at him with each step and his heart began to pound.

The music from the speakers began to grow louder. Now more distorted than ever, it seem to mock them, taunt them. The snow nipped at their heels as they ran and swirled around the two boys, blocking their vision, and making it difficult for them to remain on their feet.

Suddenly, the snow and wind tapered off. The boys stopped for a moment to catch their breath and for Josh to massage his ankle. Cautiously, they looked around and as the snow gradually ceased and the moonlight returned, they discovered that they were now completely surrounded by snowmen. There was no way out!

"Winks, hand me the bag!" Josh shouted. Winks did as instructed and Josh reached in and yanked the hand axe from the sack. "Get behind me! We're going through."

Winks grasped the back of Josh's jacket as Josh limped toward the nearest snowman. His determination was evident even behind the mask of snow and ice on his face. "I'm going to hack one of these bastards down, Winks, and when I do we hightail it to shore, got me?"

"Okay, Josh," Winks replied in a jittery voice.

Josh raised the ax over his head and approached the snowmen. He took short steps toward one of the smaller ones knowing that if necessary he could force his way past it. But the moon again dipped behind the clouds and in the darkness he couldn't see the puddle of water that was slowly forming in his path. Josh was slightly off balance with Winks holding on to the back of his jacket, but when his foot reached the water it immediately slid out from under him and he crashed to the surface.

"Aaarrrrgghhhh!" he screamed as his ankle twisted and the pain shot up his leg. He reached out and grabbed it as tears rolled down his face. It felt as if his leg was on fire.

With Winks' help, he managed to climb up on one knee to massage the injured area. "I can still walk!" he shouted to Winks. "C'mon!" Josh reached down and picked up the ax but saw that the dark figures were even closer. As the moon reappeared, he saw that the circle was tightening and the snowmen had begun to change.

No longer were the snowmen carrying artificial instruments. Now in their snowy taloned hands were knives, sabers, and clubs. There were snowmen with eye patches, pockmarks, scars, and rotted crutches. But what unnerved him the most was the sight of his own snowman, the Lead Snowman, now in among the others. Black trails running down it's face, an ax in place of the gold baton.

Although fueled by rage and determined to go on, the horror of his situation was banging on the backdoor of his consciousness demanding to be let in. Josh took a couple of deep breaths trying to control his own welling panic. He could feel Winks' hands shaking as he held tight to the back of his jacket. Was there another way out? Josh looked around and saw that there was not. And somehow they had gotten even closer.

Josh attempted a single step forward but his ankle screamed and sent a bolt of fire straight through to his groin. He could feel his grip on the ax weakening. It was as if he had somehow sprung a leak and all of his strength was pouring out onto the ice.

He slipped down to one knee, the pain blurring his vision. He squinted through tears so he wouldn't lose sight of the snowmen. He gritted his teeth, sat down, and tried to loosen the laces to ease the pressure on his injured ankle. He began to shiver and couldn't catch his breath. Black spots began to swirl before his eyes as his vision slowly weakened and grew fuzzy. His eyelids felt as if weights had been put on them and he could no longer feel the tips of his fingers. Darkness closed in from all sides. He tried desperately to remain conscious knowing that if he passed out now, he would certainly never awaken.

Winks grabbed Josh by the front of his jacket and pulled him close. He wrapped his arms under Josh's shoulders and gently dragged him to the center of the surrounding snowmen. The warmth of Winks' body brought the shivering under control enough for Josh to catch his breath. But as his sight began to clear he saw the snowmen were now no more than ten feet away and the Lead Snowman was even closer with an ax held high over its head.

Josh looked at Winks and turned over the hand axe. "You still got a chance, pal," he whispered. "Over on the right, there's a space small enough for you to slip through. But you have to move fast. Just keep swinging as you run. Don't let anything stop you."

Winks' began shaking. "I can't leave you. I can't leave you here alone, Josh!" Tears were running down the younger boy's face. "I won't do it! I won't do it!"

With that, Winks tightened his grip around the hand axe and charged straight at the Lead Snowman, not taking his eyes off him for a second. "Son of a bitch! Son of a bitch!" he screamed and plunged the ax directly into the Lead Snowman's chest.

The wind howled and snow began to whirl madly around him. Winks was lifted up into the air and flung backward. He fell onto the ice, face first, breaking his nose. The pain jerked him into a fetal position. As he placed his palms to his face, the Lead Snowman's ax slammed into the ice exactly where his legs had been only a second before.

32

When Mike Shays spoke to his son at the Campbell home, he, like Winks, wasn't being completely honest. Although he had said he expected to be released within a few hours, in actuality, his paperwork was already being processed. Twenty minutes later he was out and, just as Winks had suspected, making his way toward the Snowman's Parade. The hat and scarf were still out there somewhere and he was going to find them.

It was a fifteen minute ride from the Municipal Center to the lake and when he made the turn onto Shore Road he was startled by the ominous clouds that hung over it. The snow was falling heavily and visibility was poor but, strangely enough, only in the area surrounding Little Pond Lake. On the ride from the Municipal Center, he hadn't seen a single snowflake yet monstrous snowdrifts had formed at the entrance of the parade and along the surrounding shoreline.

He pulled the truck over near the concession stands, reached behind the seat into the toolbox, and pulled out his flashlight.

Climbing out of the truck and then onto its hood, Mike shone its powerful beam on the lake in the hope of catching a glimpse of Walks' clothing blowing around somewhere out there. Since the lake and the Snowman's Parade were several feet below the sidewalk, he was able to see past the snow barriers, but not much further. He searched for several minutes but came up empty. That's when he heard how bizarre the music coming from the speakers sounded. Surely Nick must have noticed it by now, he thought.

Although the flashlight beam wasn't powerful enough to reach the ice shack, the overhead spotlights on the speaker columns did make it possible for it to be made out. When he looked closely, he saw that the ice shack was almost completely covered in snow. There was a dull glow emanating from it but if anyone was inside, it was clear that they were in for the night.

The snowdrifts were now at least eight feet high in every direction and there didn't appear to be any openings. He shut off the flashlight, climbed back in the truck, and drove along Shore Road hoping to find at least one area low enough to climb over and get out on the ice. That's when he noticed the pier.

The pier was used during the summer months as a dock for the motorboats and in winter as a place to refuel the snowmobiles and ATV's. Since a gasoline pump had been installed on the end of the pier, the area was wired with heating coils to keep it free from ice and snow.

He pulled the truck over to the front of it, and was delighted to see that it was the only entrance to the lake not blocked by the huge columns of snow. Mike turned off the engine, picked up the flashlight, got out, and carefully ventured across the wooden planks.

When he reached the end of the pier, he turned on the beam and tried to bring the parade into view. But it was no use. The falling snow was too thick and he couldn't see more than a few yards.

"Ahhh! This is a waste of time," Mike said. "Might as well go to the Campbells', pick up Theodore, and come back first thing in the morning." He reached into his pocket for his keys and turned toward the truck when he heard glass shatter. He spun around and looked back out on the ice. Under the spotlights he saw something moving near the ice shack. Nick Pederuco had broken the glass and was trying to climb out of the window. Nick was not a large man but the window appeared to be too small even for someone with his slight frame.

Seeing that he might be in trouble, he called out. "Hey, Nick," Mike shouted. "Are you all right? Do you need any help?"

Nick's head turned toward the sound of the voice. "Mike?" he called back. "Mike Shays, is that you?"

"It's me, Nick," he replied shouting over the increasing sound of the wind. "Are you in trouble?"

"Mike, listen to me!" Nick replied at the top of his voice. "Your kid's out there! He might be in trouble. I saw him with Josh Campbell, but that was a while ago. You got to get them!"

Nick didn't have to tell him twice. He was about to jump down on the ice but decided the truck would be faster. True, the flatbed would probably be damaged after that four-foot drop from the pier's end to the lake's surface, but that didn't matter. His boy was out there!

Climbing in, Mike started the engine and threw the truck into gear. He jumped the sidewalk and steered onto the pier itself. Anticipating the drop at the end, he slammed the pedal to the floor and the truck raced over the wooden planks toward the lake.

Although Mike didn't realize it, the danger was not from the weight of the truck but from the pier itself. The heating coils had done their job in melting the snow but the planks were soaking wet and small patches of ice had formed. As he thundered across, the wheels struck one of those patches and threw the truck into a skid. Mike finally regained control but not soon enough to avoid hitting the gas pump, which ripped from its underpinnings and fell to the ice as the truck flew from the pier and onto the lake.

Gasoline spewed from the broken pump and emptied all over the ice. Mike saw the damage from his rearview mirror but was far too concerned about Winks to care.

With the high beams reflecting off the snow he was able to make out shadows ahead that slowly revealed themselves as the snowmen lined up in a circle.

"What the hell??!" he said. But when the headlights reflected off the demonic silhouette of the Lead Snowman, complete with Walks' hat and scarf, he forgot about everything else, gunned the engine, and charged.

Josh crawled over, grabbed Winks by the back of his coat, and dragged the smaller boy toward him. There had to be a way out. But how? That's when he saw the headlights speeding toward them.

"Get ready to move, Winks!" Josh shouted and ignoring the pain, staggered to his feet. Winks looked behind him and saw the lights as well. The adrenaline racing through his system made him forget about his broken nose and he immediately slipped his shoulder under Josh's arm. He knew his friend had only one good leg and if he needed a crutch, well, a crutch he would be.

There was a sound like a baseball bat hitting a large rug, then suddenly chunks of snow were flying all around them. Winks helped Josh move to the side as five of the snowmen, including the Lead Snowman, exploded before their eyes. The truck spun 180 degrees and came to a halt, it's grill now facing the shore.

The passenger side door swung open. "Get in!! Get in now!!"

Mike shouted.

Using Winks for support Josh hobbled to the truck and both boys climbed in.

Mike pulled the door closed behind them. He took a quick look at the two and was startled by their condition. He immediately turned the heater up to full.

"Good Lord!" he said. "You boys look terrible. Theodore! What happened to your nose?"

Winks took a deep breath. "I dink I busted it. But I'b ball right Dhad."

"You broke your nose?! How on earth…."

Winks quickly shook his head and helped Josh prop his leg on the dashboard.

"Josh?" Mike asked.

Josh slid back in his seat, ripped off his gloves, and began loosening the laces on his boot. "I messed up my ankle," he said as the pain in his leg lessened. "I don't think it's broken but it's sprained real bad."

Mike stared at the two boys for a moment. "What were you two doing out here, especially after all that's happened?"

Winks looked at his father, shoved his hands in his pockets, pulled out a handkerchief, and blew his nose. A sharp pain split across the side of his face. He winced but discovered that with the blood and snot cleared out, he could breathe normally again. He returned the bloody wad to his pocket and then turned back to his father.

"We're out here because of dat," he said pointing to the remaining snowmen. "Walks killed Josh's granddad, Teo McKay, and Mr. Allison. I knew youb be coming here tonight and I wasn't going to leb him get you too dhad. I just wasn't."

"What…What is this nonsense? What do you know about

Lucas Walks?" Mike sputtered.

"I know everyting," Winks replied flatly and then pulled out the handkerchief to dab his nose.

It was at that moment that Mike Shays felt a sense of remorse greater than any he had ever felt in his life. For so long he thought of Winks as a good kid but nothing special. He had long given up any dreams of his son becoming a star quarterback, class president, or an Olympic athlete. Theodore was a comic book fanatic, a computer nerd, a dreamer. Now here was his ten-year-old son risking his life to protect him from an act he committed thirty years ago. No, it wasn't remorse he was feeling, it was shame.

Just then, Winks reached for the door.

"Where are you going?" Mike shouted as he grabbed the boy's arm.

"Da hat and scarf dab!" he shouted back. "I'b got to destroy da hat and scarf!"

"No!!" Mike replied shaking his head. "That's something I have to do."

As he reached for the door handle, Josh put his hand on Mike's chest, signaling him to stop. "Mr. Shays," he said pointing to an area about thirty yards in front of the truck, "I think you better have a look."

Mike glanced at Josh and then to the place where he was pointing. "That…That can't be. It can't be! It isn't possible!"

But it was. At the furthest reach of the truck headlights stood the Lead Snowman, once again fully attired in the band uniform complete with the hat and scarf. And as the moon reflected off the ice, the three of them could see the black trails running down the sides of its face and the brown and yellow icicles pulled back in a hideous, sadistic grin.

Mike stared at it and felt the rage well up inside him.

Walks did it. He's come back to get his revenge just like he swore he would.

Mike gunned the accelerator and released the clutch. The truck lurched forward over the fresh snow and picked up speed. The grinning white hulk stood motionless as they raced toward it. But they had driven only a few yards when the truck mysteriously went out of control and began to spin. Mike quickly downshifted and brought it to a stop.

"No problem," he said. "We'll try again, only a little slower this time." He put the truck back in gear and gently pressed down on the accelerator. The wheels spun but the truck did not move. He tried again with the same results. He popped open the door, looked down, and discovered the wheels were embedded in a large patch of slush created by the remains of the snowmen he had destroyed. He put the truck into reverse but that didn't work either.

Mike shifted into first, then reverse, then back again, hoping that the wheels might catch and pull them free.

There was a sharp cracking sound and Mike and Josh turned toward their windows. Several cracks had formed in the ice beneath them.

Mike shot out his arm to grab Winks and Josh when they heard a loud snapping sound. The truck slumped backward as if one of the rear tires had gone flat. There was another loud cracking sound but before they could react, they were thrown backward as the rear of the truck fell through the ice and the front lifted up off the surface and into the air. It then shook, pitched to one side, and began to sink.

Josh was thrown against the passenger side door and Winks slid into him. Leaning back and using his elbows for leverage, Josh pressed against the window and tried to push himself up. At the same time, Winks grabbed the steering wheel and pulled himself toward his father.

Josh turned and saw that his side of the truck was completely submerged. And from the dark waters, what looked to be skeletal hands appeared and pressed against the glass. Josh gasped as they began to wrap around the door handle. Josh immediately slammed the lock down and climbed upwards toward the driver's door.

Mike had forced the door open and was climbing out. He planted himself on the doorframe, grabbed Winks' arm and pulled him out of the truck. Winks wasted no time and launched himself from the vehicle onto the ice. Now Mike had a firm grip on Josh and was pulling him up, when suddenly a skeletal arm smashed through the passenger window and grabbed the boy's bad leg.

Josh howled in pain but kept his grip. Mike planted his shoulder against the doorframe and stood, pulling the boy up with him as the waters quickly rushed in. Josh lashed out with his good leg and managed to break free from the skeletal grasp.

The truck was sinking rapidly. Mike pulled Josh into his arms and dove to the surface. The impact sent them both sprawling, but fortunately neither was hurt.

When they climbed to their feet, they saw that they were once again almost completely surrounded by snowmen.

"We better move or we're done for!" Josh shouted.

"That way!" Winks said pointing to the only opening.

Mike wrapped his arm under Josh's shoulder and the three of them ran toward the gap in the surrounding snowmen toward the pier.

Josh glanced up at the sky and saw that the dark clouds were growing thicker and were descending on the lake.

A fog dimmed the lights from Shore Road but in the background they could hear the music from the parade continue to play.

"I can't see da pier anymore," Winks shouted.

"Wait! Wait!" Josh said. "I hear something. Listen!"

They stopped running for a second and heard the distinctive sound of the ice cracking around them.

"With all this damn noise I can't tell which direction it's coming from," Mike said.

Winks spun his head around. "Behine us! It's cubbing fom behine us."

"C'mon!!" Mike yelled and they ran as fast as they could into the fog that covered the pier and their only means of escape.

33

It was Winks who first noticed the gasoline. It wasn't so much the smell (he couldn't smell because of his broken nose), but the way the fumes irritated the sensitive skin inside his nostrils. "Dis way, dis way!" he said leading the others. The sound of the cracking ice followed them like a shark honing in on the smell of blood. "The pier canb't be more den a few yards ahead."

He prayed he was right but he had no real way of knowing. The fog had descended like a curtain and the snow was falling steadily. Suddenly there was a clap of thunder and a bolt of lightning flashed across the dark skies.

The thunder again pierced the air, this time so loudly they could feel the shockwaves through the ice beneath them. But it was the lightning that previewed the danger ahead.

The snowmen had massed in front of them, blocking the pier.

They stopped. There was nowhere to go. No way off the ice. The thunder was continuously rumbling. The lightning began to flash faster and faster in an almost strobe-like fashion. The sounds of the ice breaking up behind them grew louder with each passing second.

It was Josh who noticed that the snowmen were absorbing the

gasoline pouring from the pier out onto the surface. He pulled out his father's lighter, knelt down, ran his finger across the ice, then put it to his lips. Just water.

"I hope this works!" he said. He spun the wheel and flung the Zippo (with its patented windproof flame) over the ice. It landed directly in front of the snowmen.

It caught immediately. Flames engulfed them, igniting the jackets, scarves, and finally the hats. There were high-pitched squealing noises as the snowmen melted.

Immediately the sound of the ice cracking stopped and the fog began to shimmer and dissipate. But Mike knew that they were still in danger.

"The fire is inching back toward the pump. C'mon!!"

Mike yanked Josh up into his arms and turned toward the ice shack. The lightning and thunder continued their display as the three ran for cover.

Please God. Just let me get the kids out of here safely. After that do with me what you want.

Almost in answer to Mike's prayer, there was an explosion as the gas tank went up and fireworks lit the sky. The force knocked them all to the ground.

"Is anyone hurt?" Mike called out as he staggered to his feet, his ears ringing like fire alarms.

Winks winced and lightly touched his nose, which had begun to bleed again. "I'b okay. How 'bout you Josh?"

Josh slowly propped his arms behind him and dragged himself up into a sitting position. "Not good. I can't move my leg."

"That's all right," Mike said reaching down and lifting him up. "I'll carry you to the ice shack. Once inside we can call for help."

As they started across the ice, the parade lights suddenly came on and in the distance they saw Nick Pederuco approaching in an ATV. This one was specifically designed to stay afloat should the ice beneath it give way. It resembled a golf cart with large studded balloon tires.

"Oh, thank God, the cavalry's here," Mike said smiling.

Within a few moments, Nick pulled up alongside. He looked wild, agitated. "Are you all right? Good Lord. The snowmen are on fire!" He seemed to be shaking as he spoke.

"The boys are hurt," Mike said repositioning Josh in his arms. "Can you take us back to the shack?"

Nick looked the three over and nodded. "Sure, sure," he replied almost too quickly. "But I can only take the boys. This thing only holds three."

Mike lowered Josh into the seat and told Winks to take the seat beside him. "Go ahead with Nick. I'll follow you to the shack on foot."

"Okay," Winks replied as Nick strapped the boys into their seatbelts.

Pederuco smiled but when Mike smiled back, an eerie sensation crawled up his spine. "Nick, are you okay?" he asked. "You seem a little…."

Nick threw the ATV in gear and sped away before Mike could finish the sentence.

Instantly Winks' gut feeling went on alert. With all the excitement, he had stopped paying attention to it.

But we're out of danger now, right? So why….

"Nick. What's dohin on?" Winks asked nervously.

"What makes you think anything is going on?" he replied defensively. "Nothing is going on, nothing at all!" The strangeness in Nick's voice caught Josh's attention. He looked over at Nick and saw the man's eyes were wide and sweat was pouring down his face even though the temperature was well below freezing.

The ATV, although slow, easily carried them across the surface toward the ice shack. As the moments passed Winks' internal warning system grew to such a fever pitch that it was almost comical. He could almost envision the robot from *Lost in Space* waving its mechanical arms shouting "Warning! Warning, Will Robinson!" Winks turned and whispered to Josh. "Someting's wrong," he said. "Someting is bery wrong."

Winks comment confirmed what he was quickly beginning to believe himself.

"Nick," Josh said. "I want you to stop this thing."

Nick tilted his head from side to side, like he was listening to instructions from some invisible headset. "Stop it?" he said turning to the boys, his eyes red and darting back and forth. "No one can stop it. No one. I've tried. Believe me I've tried to stop it." Tears began rolling down his face. "But you can't stop it. The lake must have its sacrifices. The lake must be fed!"

Winks spun around and saw his father fading into the distance. He quickly yanked at his seatbelt but his gloves were wet and he couldn't grip the release catch.

"Dhad!" he shouted.

The word had no sooner left his lips when a wall of flame shot across the ice blocking Mike's path.

"Josh, I can't oben da damn seatbelt!" he shouted in panic.

Josh looked back at Mike and then at Nick expecting him to turn the ATV around. But Nick's condition was rapidly deteriorating. He had his head tilted back and he was singing, no, shouting a song at the top of his lungs while pounding the steering wheel in time to the rhythm. He ignored Josh's stare and continued to bellow as if he were in the cart by himself. Josh had seen enough. It was clear that the head of the DPW was either drunk or completely out of his mind.

The wind howled and sleet sprayed their faces, stinging their eyes. Josh gave a knowing look at Winks, then leaned against him and slowly braced his good leg against the floor. Then he turned back toward Nick.

Nick was not that much bigger but he was strong, so there wouldn't be any second chances. Fortunately, Nick's seatbelt wasn't connected so, after taking a deep breath, Josh lunged at him and shoved Nick from the ATV.

Josh saw Nick's eyes widen and mouth a desperate "NO!!" as he fell to the ice and tumbled across the surface like a rag doll.

Josh snapped off his belt, slid into the driver's seat, and turned the ATV around.

At fifty-seven years of age, tired, wet, and frozen nearly to the bone, Mike was in no condition to run after the ATV even though he knew he had made a mistake leaving the boys with Nick. His breath was coming in heavy gasps and a stitch jabbed his side. He picked up his pace as best he could when the fire flashed across the path before him.

He put up his arms to shield his face. Then peering at the fire through his spread fingers, he stared in disbelief at what was beginning to form in front of him. The flames were melding together, changing shape from a wall into a spire. Slowly it began to spin.

It positioned itself in front of Mike forcing him to back up and move further out on the ice. Mike watched as a figure gradually took shape inside the funnel. Its eyes were red hot like the burning coals they were and licks of fire formed jagged teeth. The eyes stared and as they did the flames grew higher. The figure continued its transformation until it took on very distinct human-like features. Features that Mike Shays had last seen thirty years ago.

"Walks!!" he shouted.

"Fasta! Josh, fasta!!" Winks shouted as Josh speeded toward Mike Shays, but this specially constructed ATV had been built for power, not speed. As Winks' father moved further out on the ice, it increased the distance between them. Although Josh had the accelerator to the floor it still seemed like they were moving in slow motion.

Mike continued to back away, carefully avoiding the area of broken ice. Half of him couldn't believe what he was seeing and the other half was bracing for an attack. He wobbled as the flames drew nearer. The wind howled and seemed to shout, "Mikey! Mikey! Mikey!" Mike slipped, then fell to the surface. The thin veil of icy cold water splashed his face and cleared his head. Realizing that he was dealing with something far beyond his ability to handle, he climbed to his feet and moved away as quickly as he could. But the column of fire in which Walks now existed followed.

I'm here, Mikey! a voice screeched inside his head. *I'm here and it's payback time!*

Winks and Josh were still too far away to do anything. Winks watched in panic as the fire figure pursued his father as he stumbled across the ice. Winks knew his dad needed a weapon. He searched around and found one in the back of his seat. It was a crowbar hidden under the blue rubber nets that were used to wrap the snowmen. He had wished for something a little more powerful, like a rocket launcher, but the crowbar would have to do.

The ATV was nearly within striking distance. Winks tore off his gloves and gripped the crowbar tightly in his hand. Now finally free of his seatbelt, he climbed up on the seat. "Get dus close enoub so I can geb this to my dhad!" Winks shouted as the snow and sleet sprayed against his face.

Josh nodded but out of the corner of his eye he saw something eerily glowing alongside the pier. At first, he thought it was a reflection of the flames, but when he looked closer he was able to make out its true shape. He turned to tell Winks but the boy had already launched himself from the ATV and was running toward his father. In seconds he was near enough to toss the crowbar to him.

Mike grabbed it with one hand and instantly swung at the flaming apparition whirling before him. The figure rippled like water inside a fish tank but sustained no injury. Mike swung again but with the same results.

Seeing this, Mike grabbed Winks and flung him as far as he could to the side as the fiery figure advanced on him. Mike continued backing away moving further and further out on the ice. The figure followed, its coal red eyes turned white hot and the wispy teeth closed into what looked like a blue circle of flame. Mike held the crowbar over his head in anticipation of whatever was to come next.

At least the boy's safe.

Walks struck. A column of fire shot out and engulfed Mike in flame.

Although neither Winks nor his father had noticed, Josh had taken off. He desperately wanted to stay and fight beside them but his leg was nearly useless now.

Besides, if the glowing object was what he thought it was, he could end this once and for all.

As he raced toward the pier his suspicions were confirmed. The hat and scarf lay against the snowdrift glowing like they had been coated in phosphorous. He pulled the ATV up alongside the snowdrift, reached down and picked them up. As he reached for the gearbox, Nick leapt over the back and grabbed him by the throat.

"Aaaggghhhhhhh!!" Mike screamed as the fire ignited his clothes and covered him in flame. He could smell his hair and eyebrows burning. The smoke stung his eyes as he flailed at the flames.

"Die Mikey! Die. Die. Die. Die. Die!!!"

Mike stumbled blindly across the surface toward the area where the ice had broken up and formed a hole.

"Dhad no!" Winks shouted and raced toward him. He plowed into his father and knocked him to the ice just before he would have fallen into the water. As his father lay near the lip of the ice hole, Winks rushed over, grabbed a large chunk of ice, and splashed water on his father. The flames died quickly. Winks dropped the ice, grabbed his dad, and turned him over. His face was partially burned and blackened by smoke. Most of his hair was gone but luckily, because of his heavy clothing, the fire hadn't soaked down to the rest of him.

"Thanks son," he said gasping and wincing from the pain. "I thought...I thought I was done for."

Winks pulled his scarf from around his neck, dipped it in the icy water, and placed it against the burned section of his father's face. Mike gasped as the water ran down and dripped inside his coat but welcomed the relief it brought. Slowly he climbed to his feet and watched as the flames shimmered and pulsed. Something was happening to it. The fire was still blazing but the figure of Walks had disappeared. But with what felt like a thousand needles jabbing him in the face, Mike was taking no chances. With Winks at his side he carefully backed around the edge of the ice hole, hoping that the water would keep the creature at bay.

Winks saw the crowbar lying on the surface a few feet away and dashed over to pick it up. His hands were shaking so badly he could barely get his fingers around it.

He hadn't said anything but he was more frightened now than he had ever been in his life. This had been too much…too much. If Walks could strike at his father like a demonic flamethrower, then he could do anything. His panic was amplified when from behind him he heard his father gasp in surprise. Winks spun around to see that skeletal hands had shot out from the ice hole and had grabbed Mike's legs.

Nick was incredibly strong. He had his fingers wrapped around Josh's neck and was dragging him backwards over the seat. "You little bastard!" Nick screamed. "You can't interfere! The lake must be fed. The lake must have its sacrifices!"

Josh had been caught completely off guard. Nick had been hiding behind one of the snowdrifts and pounced on him as soon as Josh picked up the hat and scarf. The boy could feel the madman's hot breath on his neck and knew that he had to act soon or this lunatic would strangle him.

As his good leg scraped along the top of the seat, he felt his house keys jab his thigh. In desperation, he reached into his pocket, wrapped his hand around them, and yanked them out. His lungs were aching from lack of oxygen and he began to feel lightheaded. He pushed the keys in between each of his fingers so they jutted out from his knuckles like Wolverine's adamantium claws. Still feeling the hot breath upon him, Josh calculated where the madman's face would be and struck!

Nick screeched in agony as blood spurted down his cheeks. Josh bent forward then flipped back ramming his head into Nick's chest. Pederuco was knocked off the ATV and crashed into the snowdrift. Slowly, he climbed to his feet but when Josh turned toward him and revved the ATV engine, Nick ran off.

After catching his breath, Josh checked around for the hat and scarf. They were still on the seat.

The pier was just ahead.

The skeletal hands had yanked Mike's feet from under him so quickly that there wasn't time for him to react. He pitched backward and his head hit the ice with an alarming thud, knocking him unconscious. The bony fingers then began to crawl up his calves and drag him into the water. Winks dove to the surface and grabbed his father's hands in his own but he was far too small and too light to prevent Mike's descent.

"Josh!" he screamed and finally noticed that Josh was nowhere to be found. The flames that contained the figure of Walks had gone out. And what appeared to be the Lead Snowman, without the hat and scarf, was now standing in its place. It was covered in black soot and the eyes were a grayish white and looked like burnt ashes, yet they continued to throb and glow.

With his one free hand, Winks used the crowbar to stab at the ice. It took several tries but he was finally able to pierce the surface enough to use the metal bar for leverage. He held tight to his father but he simply wasn't strong enough. He felt his hands loosen on both his father and the crowbar.

"Josh! Josh!" he yelled. "Where are you?!"

In the distance, Winks heard the Emergency Service sirens go off. Someone must have seen the fire on the pier. Help would soon be on the way. Pain knifed through Winks' arm as his father was pulled another few inches. He felt like he was being torn in half.

This isn't working.

The clarity of that single thought startled Winks. He wasn't giving up but he suddenly discovered that he was no longer afraid. The fact that he was now facing the most dangerous situation of his life and wasn't afraid was so alien to him that he almost laughed.

The human brain is very much like a computer, his teacher told him. I guess, he thought, that must be true. When his computer at home could no longer process all the information being loaded into it, it simply stopped and rebooted itself. With his new-found sense of calm, it seemed that's exactly what his brain had done. It could no longer handle the fear and simply shut that part of itself off.

Winks was startled out of his revelation by another pull. It was true. This wasn't working but he had an idea what might.

There was gasoline burning everywhere and the winds were especially strong as they snaked across the pier. He could hear the burning wood pop and hiss as he drew closer. Josh had the hat and scarf pressed tightly against his chest. Twice the winds had almost ripped them from his hands. He knew that he couldn't simply toss them into the flames for they would surely blow back to their owner. No. He was going to have to make sure they were secured in one spot until they were incinerated.

The only place Josh saw that could serve this purpose was the jagged base of the gasoline pump. The twisted metal reached out from the pier's edge like blackened claws. Once he had the hat and scarf jammed down onto those spikes all the wind in hell wasn't going to rip them free.

There had been two explosions already and he knew the fire trucks were on their way. The tarry smoke burned his eyes and lungs. The heat would have been enough to stop any sane man. But these were insane times.

"Responsibility, Josh, that's the key," he heard his grandfather say.

"Responsibility." Josh said aloud and turned the ATV into the flames.

Inch by inch Winks slipped the crowbar from the ice. If his plan were to work, he would have to move fast. His fingers were numb and it was getting harder to maintain his grip. "Wake up dhad!" he shouted again and again but his father was clearly knocked cold. The forked end of the crowbar was coming into view. He would have one shot and one shot only but his mind was clear. He could do this.

And he did. As the bar came loose Winks dove toward the ice hole. With his left hand he grabbed his father's belt to prevent him from sliding into the water, and with his right slammed the crowbar down on the wrists of the skeletal hands as they tightened around his father's thighs.

If it weren't for the fact that Josh's face was sopping wet and his jacket hood was pulled down closely against his head, his face might have been burned as badly as Mike's. Fortunately, he still had what was left of his goggles dangling around his neck so he pulled them over his eyes, then wrapped his scarf across his mouth.

He held his breath as he drove into the flames but he had gotten only a few feet before greasy smoke and soot covered the goggles. He was beginning to think that he wasn't going to make it when he found himself in a small area where the flames had dwindled and the winds had blown back the smoke. He took another deep breath, cleaned the lenses, and continued toward the twisted metal.

This area, however, was not so protected. Tiny sparks caught in his scarf and were threatening to ignite. He yanked it from his face but the intense heat made his lips curl back in pain. He pressed his gloved hand over the exposed area and continued toward the edge of the pier. With flames licking all around him, he saw the jagged metal of what remained of the pump and raced toward it. As he tried to pull up alongside, the wet ice caused the ATV to spin and slam into the fiery pylons, throwing Josh across the seat. His leg twisted and the pain re-announced its position in the scheme of things.

With fire on all sides and the wood of the pylons popping and hissing like steaks on a barbecue, Josh wrapped the hat and scarf into a ball and jammed them down over the metal spire. They caught instantly and turned into a ball of flame.

34

The moment Winks struck the skeletal arms, they disintegrated into dust and drifted down to the surface of the water. He braced his legs against the side of the ice hole, hooked his arm under his father's shoulder, and tried to pull him out. Having been dragged nearly halfway in, Mike's waterlogged clothes nearly doubled his weight. Winks pulled valiantly but his father barely budged.

Winks' gut feeling kicked in again. Something was happening, but what? If the snowmen were to stage another attack, they were done for. With his father unconscious and his own energy reserve on empty there was no way they could defend themselves.

As Winks held his father, he felt the ice shudder and saw the water inside the ice hole begin to ripple. He took a quick look at the snowman but it appeared dead. And the pier, although still aflame and covered in smoke, did not look any different than before.

What's going on?

Then he felt the tremor again. This time it was stronger and the sudden movement almost caused him to lose his grip on his father.

Josh, where are you?

Josh saw that the canopy over the ATV had ignited. He

switched the gears to reverse and sped backward out of the flames. He was coughing and gasping for air and his jacket was blackened with soot, yet he kept his eye on the flaming hat and scarf. Pieces of ash had broken free and were floating into the sky above.

Finally clear, he brought the ATV to a stop and attempted to catch his breath. Slowly he began to smile.

It's over! It's finally over.

That's when he felt the ice begin to shake.

Acting almost purely on instinct, he hit the gas, backed the ATV around, and looked out on the surface for Winks and his dad. The reflections of the flames made it difficult for him to see. He prayed that they had somehow made it back to the shore but couldn't leave it to chance. He had to be sure.

When he reached down to the gearbox, he saw for the first time that the ATV had four gears, not three. At the top was written the word low, under it drive, neutral, and, finally, reverse.

Had he been driving in the low gear all along?

He slipped the shift into the second slot. The one marked drive. He pressed down on the accelerator and was jerked back by the sudden increase of speed. Within seconds, he was traveling at twice what the ATV had been able to manage before. "Hold on, Winks!" he shouted. "Hold on!"

Winks was clearly losing the battle. His father was slipping into the water, his own clothes were sopping wet, and his fingers numb. But he refused to admit defeat.

Josh will be back.

Josh was his hero and he would be back. But more than that, Josh was his friend. And he knew that his friend would never desert him.

He looked down through teary eyes and saw his small hands, now a noticeable shade of blue, wrapped tightly around his father's belt. He wasn't giving up. No matter what. Even if he died here, he wasn't giving up. He gritted his teeth and pulled harder and then, right in the middle of what seemed to be a hopeless situation, a feeling of reassurance came over him.

Maybe you have what it takes to be a hero after all.

It was at that moment he saw Josh roaring from the smoke and toward him in the ATV, its canopy aflame and flapping in the wind. His heart did two somersaults and his resolve doubled.

I knew you wouldn't run out on me, Josh. I just knew it!

Within seconds, Josh was sliding to a stop near the ice hole. "What happened?"

"Walks set my fadher on fire and den dis *ting*...reached out from da lake and tried to pull hib in. I taught we were finished bud for some readin da snowman just went dead. Look for yourself. It's just standing dere."

"I think I know why," Josh replied. "I found the hat and scarf and jammed them down on one of the spikes from the broken gas pump. They're burning up."

"All right!" Winks said beaming with excitement. "But howb are we goin to get my dhad out da here?"

Without saying a word, Josh turned the ATV around and backed it up toward the ice hole. He reached back and flung the blue rubber netting to Winks. "Wrap this under your father's arms. Then I'll pull him out."

A huge smile leapt to Winks face. He grabbed the netting and quickly followed Josh's directions.

Josh slipped the gearbox to the low setting and gently tapped the accelerator. The wheels slipped and caught a few times but slowly Josh pulled Mike Shays from the water.

As the ATV gently pulled him onto the ice, his eyes fluttered, then opened.

"Dhad!" Winks exclaimed. "You're all right!"

Mike seemed confused but was able to stagger to his feet with Winks' help.

"Get him inside," Josh directed as the wind ripped the fiery canopy from the roof and sent it sailing across the ice.

Winks slowly unwrapped his father from the netting and helped him in. Then he sat down next to him and strapped the seatbelts around them both.

As Josh was hauling the net back into the ATV, the surface began to rumble like an earthquake. The ice surrounding them began to crack and shudder. Winks turned to Josh, hoping his friend knew what to do.

He did. With everyone in the ATV, Josh switched to drive and jammed the accelerator to the floor. As he sped past the Lead Snowman, it toppled over and quickly began to dissolve. Josh had no sooner taken his eyes off it when a piece of ice, the size of a manhole cover, disappeared into the lake several feet in front of them. Josh swerved but the rear tire slammed against the lip causing the back of the vehicle to bounce a foot or so into the air.

Josh winced as his bad leg slapped against the dashboard, but the wide cracks that were appearing all over the surface became the more immediate problem.

Large areas were caving in while others exploding upwards forcing Josh to zigzag around the holes. Lightning struck one of the pine trees on the Allison property and split it in half. The explosion echoed across the lake as the tremors grew more powerful. Water was rapidly covering the ice, making it more difficult for Josh to steer. On several occasions, the ATV slid, teetered from side to side, and nearly tipped over. Another explosion sent water and chunks of ice raining down on them. Shaking the spray from his face, Josh held tight and continued toward the shore.

As the ATV bounced over the jagged terrain, Josh was desperately trying to figure a way to get off the lake. The pier was still on fire and the lake was fenced in on all sides by drifts eight to ten feet high. There was no way they could climb over those barriers to the street. Not in the condition he and Mike were in. But with the ice breaking up all around them, it was only a matter of time before the surface disappeared completely.

Josh felt his heart sink. After all this, they were trapped. It looked as if Lucas Walks, although now most certainly gone, would get his revenge after all.

"Josh look!" Winks shouted.

Josh did and saw the front end of the pier collapse onto the lake. The pylons, weakened by the fire, had finally given way.

"Hold tight!" Josh shouted and roared toward the flaming ramp. He had no idea whether it would hold their weight but it was the only way out.

The music from the parade grew stranger and louder. The steering wheel shook in Josh's hands as if it was alive. An explosion jettisoned a skeleton from the icy water. It spun in the air then tumbled to the surface several yards in front of them. Josh swerved around it as the vibrations of several more explosions nearly flipped the ATV over on its side.

"Fasta, Josh, fasta," Winks shouted as he wrapped his arms around his father.

In the reflection of the firelight, Josh saw that where the pier had fallen to the surface, the surrounding ice had melted away. With only seconds to make a decision, Josh had to calculate if they had enough speed to skim across the few feet of water to the ramp. The pier extended nearly twenty feet from the sidewalk to the lake. If the ATV didn't make it they would sink into at least ten feet of icy water. He and Mike would never get out in time. Josh eased his foot off the accelerator when Winks, seeing what lay ahead, turned and shouted, "Ba-oon tires Josh!" pointing to the wheels.

Suddenly remembering that this was an ATV specially made to stay afloat, Josh slammed his foot back down on the accelerator. Keeping his fingers crossed, the machine reached top speed and skidded across the surface like a flat rock. Slush and water sprayed all around until they hit the ramp.

Racing up through the flames, the wooden slats creaked and snapped behind them then disintegrated into shards and fell into the water. Josh kept the accelerator jammed to the floor until they reached the top of the pier where the machine became airborne and flew out toward the street.

The fire trucks and EMS vehicles were just arriving as the ATV soared over the sidewalk and bounced several times before sliding to a stop. All three were shaken but unhurt. Winks snapped off his seatbelt and jumped from the machine to wave down an EMS van to take care of his father and his friend.

There was another explosion as speaker columns shook, then fell into the water, silencing the bizarre, twisted music at last. Blue neon veins of electricity danced across the ice illuminating the remains of the band jackets and plastic instruments that were now slowly sinking beneath the waves. The gasoline generator exploded, taking the ice shack and tool shed with it in an eruption of wood and glass. Flaming embers turned the ticket booth into a bonfire that roared into the black and blue clouds above. The light tower squealed and exploded, then sank beneath the surface. Within minutes, all that remained of the Snowman's Parade rapidly disappeared as the lake water began to churn and bubble like lava in a volcano.

As the emergency service vehicles turned their searchlights on the lake, they were horrified to see a number of bodies in various states of decomposition slowly float to the surface. Because of the lake's low oxygen content, centuries of decay had been staved off. Flesh still clung to many of the long dead victims and almost all were covered in the clothes they wore when they met their fate. Long strands of hair dangled from rotting scalps, eyeless sockets peered back from drawn yellowed skulls, blackened teeth reflected hideous knowing grins, and skeletal arms reached out to the sky as if giving thanks for having been finally granted salvation.

Amid the spinning red and blue lights of the emergency vehicles, Josh was put on a gurney and lifted into the EMS van. Just before the doors closed, he looked out over the lake and almost smiled. Now that the hat and scarf were nothing more than blackened ash illuminated by a small dwindling flame, there was no reason to fear. It was over.

The End of the Story

In the hours that followed, over two hundred bodies in various stages of decay floated to the surface. As the remaining EMS and other emergency vehicles' spotlights swept the icy waters, crowds gathered (having been alerted by the explosions and the sirens), and gaped in awe as the lake partially re-froze around the corpses. The EMS made several attempts to remove the bodies but the surface remained too unstable to support their weight.

By morning, the area was swamped with newspaper and television news teams who nearly fell over each other to record the grizzly event. They dubbed it "The Holiday Horror" and the pictures and videos taken there were shown not only across the country but around the world. Countless scientists were interviewed to explain the phenomenon and their theories ranged from earthquake activity to geothermal fissures to secret government experiments.

The official story was that the two boys had been snowmobiling on the lake and were met by Mr. Shays. While on the ice the tremors started, forcing them to abandon their vehicles and run to the street. When they saw that snowdrifts blocked off the sidewalk, they grabbed the ATV and used the collapsed pier as their ticket off the ice.

Nick Pederuco, too, survived the ordeal, having climbed over the snowdrifts to safety. Unfortunately, when met by the EMS teams he was babbling incoherently and had to be remanded to the state psychiatric hospital for observation. He soon regained the vision in his damaged right eye and upon recovery, quietly sold his house and moved to Florida. He never told anyone what had really happened that night. Many people believed he no longer knew.

As for Mike Shays, he recovered from his burns with only minor scars and the charges regarding Ernie, Morris, and Theo were dropped. He returned to his job at Milkways and often visited the graves of his friends.

Winks underwent surgery for his broken nose and was elated to discover that the doctors were able to repair his droopy eyelid as well. When he returned to school, his classmates immediately noticed the change in him. It wasn't just the eye but the way he radiated confidence and self-assuredness.

The bullies saw this too and left him alone, preferring to pick on kids whom, if pushed, wouldn't push back. Winks kept the nickname, though, it was still better than Thee-o-dore.

Josh was in a cast for a couple of weeks and his leg eventually healed. During his recovery, he kept expecting his parents to ask him why he had lied and snuck down to the lake, but surprisingly they never brought it up. Instead, on the day the doctors removed his cast, they presented him with a new snowmobile. "It's the same make and model as the one Mike Shays just bought for Theodore," Roy said. "Since yours sank to the bottom of the lake, your mother and I took some of the money my father left us and bought you a new one."

As Josh sat down inside the new machine, he was overwhelmed with guilt and decided not to accept it. His snowmobile didn't simply sink, he wrecked it and lied about what happened. Just as he was about to open his mouth, his father walked over, placed his hand on Josh's shoulder, and handed him the keys. "We're proud of you, son," he said, "and I know your grandfather would be too." When he looked up, he could see that his parents already knew the whole story and understood.

As for the Snowman's Parade, well, it was over. All the snowmen had been destroyed, and with the national coverage of the dead floating on Little Pond Lake, any attempt at resurrecting the family event was doomed to failure. However, tourism in Sparks was far from finished. As it is with human nature, some quick-thinking entrepreneurs on the Parade Committee saw an opportunity to capitalize on the situation and made plans to replace the Snowman's Parade with the Holiday Horror.

Using state disaster relief money, they created books, videos, coffee cups, ashtrays, and other souvenirs to commemorate the event. A special museum was built and the remains of the bodies that had floated to the surface were displayed in glass booths. As gruesome as it seemed, people came in numbers equaling that of the Snowman's Parade and Sparks continued to thrive.

As for Josh and Winks, the two boys remained close and spent many happy hours snowmobiling together throughout the Adirondack Mountains. After that night on Little Pond Lake, Winks stopped looking up to Josh as his hero. He was more than that now, he was his friend.

ABOUT THE AUTHOR

Zackary Richards was born in the Bronx and presently resides in upstate New York.